THE ORANGE HOUSES

PAUL GRIFFIN

speak
An Imprint of Penguin Group (USA) Inc.

SPEAK

Published by the Penguin Group

Penguin Group (USA) Inc., 345 Hudson Street, New York, New York 10014, U.S.A.

Penguin Group (Canada), 90 Eglinton Avenue East, Suite 700, Toronto, Ontario, Canada M4P 2Y3
(a division of Pearson Penguin Canada Inc.)

Penguin Books Ltd, 80 Strand, London WC2R 0RL, England

Penguin Ireland, 25 St Stephen's Green, Dublin 2, Ireland (a division of Penguin Books Ltd)

Penguin Group (Australia), 250 Camberwell Road, Camberwell, Victoria 3124, Australia
(a division of Pearson Australia Group Pty Ltd)

Penguin Books India Pvt Ltd, 11 Community Centre, Panchsheel Park, New Delhi - 110 017, India

Penguin Group (NZ), 67 Apollo Drive, Rosedale, Auckland 0632, New Zealand
(a division of Pearson New Zealand Ltd.)

Penguin Books (South Africa) (Pty) Ltd, 24 Sturdee Avenue,
Rosebank, Johannesburg 2196, South Africa

Registered Offices: Penguin Books Ltd, 80 Strand, London WC2R 0RL, England

First published in the United States of America by Dial Books,
a division of Penguin Group (USA) Inc., 2009
Published by Speak, an imprint of Penguin Group (USA) Inc., 2011

5 7 9 10 8 6 4

Copyright © Paul Griffin, 2009
Photos by Paul Griffin and Robyn Meshulam
All rights reserved

THE LIBRARY OF CONGRESS HAS CATALOGED THE DIAL BOOKS EDITION AS FOLLOWS:
Griffin, Paul, date.
The Orange Houses / Paul Griffin.
p. cm.
Summary: Tamika, a fifteen-year-old hearing-impaired girl, Jimmi, an eighteen-year-old veteran who
stopped taking his antipsychotic medication, and sixteen-year-old Fatima, an illegal immigrant from
Africa, meet and connect in their Bronx, New York, neighborhood, with devastating results.
ISBN: 978-0-8037-3346-6 (hc)
[1. Interpersonal relations—Fiction. 2. Hearing impaired—Fiction. 3. Veterans—Fiction.
4. Mental illness—Fiction. 5. Illegal aliens—Fiction. 6. Africans—United States—Fiction.
7. Bronx (New York, N.Y.)—Fiction.] I. Title.
PZ7.G8813594Or 2009
[Fic]—dc22
2008046259

Speak ISBN 978-0-14-241982-3

Book design by Jasmin Rubero
Set in Garamond 3

Printed in the United States of America

THe OraNge Houses

You're my angel, bomb blast bright,
No slight heaven, no minor light.
You are the way,
The truth,
The light.

How you love me, girl,
The world a swirl,
No way,
No truth,
No light?

Will you still love me,
When you find out I true be,
Outside humanity,
Lost with a fire's need,

A man from sands,
Forsaken plans,
No bonds or bands,
The Devil's hands?

Only you, child, can save me.

—Jimmi Sixes

James Semprevivo changed his name to Jimmi Sixes when he came back from the desert, but most folks called him Crazy Jimmi. His military service ended with a mandatory discharge—honorable—after army psychiatrists determined he was incapable of carrying out his duties. He'd enlisted at seventeen, shipped out his eighteenth birthday and was sent home six months later.

What follows here happened a few months after Jimmi came home, shortly before he was supposed to turn nineteen. He sketched this rhyme into a newspaper margin, then whispered it to the rats that shared his cave so as not to wake his friend fifteen-year-old Tamika Sykes, sleeping restlessly in the stove light but not bleeding anymore. She'd been cut bad. Jimmi's other friend Fatima Espérer was aboveground but in no less danger.

An hour after Jimmi wrote the poem the vigilantes hung him.

chapter 1
TAMIKA

Bronx West, a high school classroom, a late October Thursday morning twenty-seven days before the hanging...

Everybody's eyes were like, Say *what?*

The teacher said the word again: "Taphophobia."

Spelling bee. Hate It scale rating: somewhere between scrubbing toilets and PMS, say 8 out of 10. The big-boned girl in the corner did not speak in front of crowds. She would write her answer on the board or be dumb. She studied the shapes made by old lady Rodriguez's mouth: Ta. Fo. Fo. Bee-ya.

Meningitis struck her ten years before, when she was five. Technically her hearing loss was "moderately severe," what lawyers looking to sue hospitals pegged 50 percent deficient. Being halfway to sound was like never being able to catch your breath.

She got by just fine when she kept her hearing aids turned on. She didn't much. The machines were what City Services could give her, old technology that jug-handled her ears and rattled her with phone and radio static, a high-pitched whir. They sharpened and dulled everything at the same time the way water will just below the surface. But turned off and plugging up her drums, the aids screened out the world. She lived for this silky silence.

"I seen more activity at sleep clinics," Teach said. "Somebody stand and deliver. Mika Sykes, save us."

Tamika rolled her eyes. *Meek*-a? Call her Mik, like *nick*.

Her thick hip caught a desk corner as she hopped over the outstretched foot of the pretty girl Shanelle just back from juvie. Word was Sha kept a box cutter tucked into her sock, its blade home-ground plastic to sneak it through the metal detector but sharp enough to slash and spill some gal's cowhide backpack last week.

Mik stabbed the blackboard with fresh chalk and spun back to her seat. She propped her head on stacked fists and closed her eyes. She was up late again last night doing her secret thing, slinking away into her dream world: drawing. Add to the no-sleep night a sugar hangover to pound the gray out of her dome. She'd washed down a box of Fig Newtons with a snuck beer. Eyes shut she saw what she drilled into the slate:

TAPHOPHOBIA
FEAR OF BEING BURIED ALIVE

At lunch another outcast bum-rushed her loner spot under the stairs. The G he called himself. So sad. He handed Mik his homework. Mik eyed the paper, algebra, held up three fingers.

"For ten questions?" The dude fished his pockets and came up with lint and dirty pennies. "All I got is a buck and some."

Mik squinted, taking in The G. Thick glasses bugged his eyes. A mouthful of metal failed to tame his buckteeth. That twisting sting pitted her stomach: repulsion, lust, both. She had a thing for losers. She grabbed the coins.

"Yo, I like y'all's braids bunched like that," he said. "Cat's ears is crazy sexy."

Mom had rolled them that morning as Mik ate breakfast—an annoying ritual. Mik fought a blush as she flipped up her phone. She clicked a hot key for a ready reply text: WUT EVR.

"Mik, lemme watch you do it, the math."

Another hot key: NOT NEVR. Last time she let him watch he faked a yawn and dropped his arm over her shoulder. So corny. She had let him brush her breast, his hand clammy and shaking. That was either too disgusting or too exciting, and she'd nailed him, elbow to ribs.

"Y'all are mad beautiful."

"Y'all are blind." The words were out before she realized she spoke them. She sounded twice as good as she thought she did, half as good as she thought she should. With her ears plugged her voice was a hollow echo trapped in her head. Stick your fingers in your ears and talk, you'll get the idea.

"Same way, slip it through my locker slot, text me after you make the drop?"

That got the BET button. She watched the player wannabe pimp limp away. Sucker would get his fool butt shot off during some bagman errand—a corpse before he hit the right to enlist. Mik blinked away that sadness and checked the boy's math. G did not stand for genius. Poor baby, she almost said.

Doing other kids' homework for small change wasn't glamorous, but she had her eye on this dope ergonomic pen that cost forty-six bucks at that Japanese bookstore downtown. She worked old-school style with Speedball ink and crow quill points. She did not dare dream the pen could be more than a hobby piece, maybe even her ticket out, a one-way escape from Mom's fate: slaving behind the Dunkin' Donuts counter when she wasn't humping the overnight restock shift at Target.

She tucked The G's buck-and-some into her pocket and started in on his algebra. The half-off discount was no sweat. She helped out when she could, but on the down low, no need to get friendly. She'd do a slow kid's math or help a blind lady cross a street. Hit and run, over and done, like that. She didn't know why she did these things. They didn't make her feel good. They didn't make her feel bad either. She couldn't figure it out.

She pulled her hair out of the bunched braids to hide her ears.

chapter 2
FATIMA

Atlantic Ocean, five miles southeast
of New York Harbor, Friday, twenty-six
days before the hanging, 3 a.m....

"Don't be afraid," the ship's mate said from the hatchway above. "Come."

The women tiptoed onto the deck as if they were treading landmined sands. For nine days they had been hiding in the backup engine room of this oil tanker fit for hauling two million barrels of light sweet crude and, this time around, thirty-four refugees. Each woman's passage cost twenty-five hundred dollars. This blind faith cash had been raised a coin at a time, person by displaced person, family by fractured African family. Those who had endured were sending their best shots at survival, if not by bloodline then heritage, west.

Of the thirty-four, most were going to Camden, where

the Immigration police did not go. Camden was written off as a city lost to drugs, prostitution and the nation's highest teen mortality rate. The rest of these travelers were going to a city somewhat safer yet no less rife with illegal employment, Atlantic City. The rest save Fatima Espérer.

Her mother had given the young woman her first name, but for her new life Fatima chose the last, a French word meaning to hope. She taught herself the language from schoolbooks that somehow escaped burning—English too. At sixteen she was headed where all told her not to go: New York. She had to visit the Statue of Liberty.

"A silly tourist trap," one of her sister travelers said.

Fatima smiled. Trap or not, she was going to see Liberty up close.

The refugees huddled at the bow, their shawls drawn tight around their heads and shoulders. The ship's mate ordered the deck lights turned off. He pointed overhead.

Fatima looked up. The night sky swung as the freighter wrestled a broken wave. The stars were nearly the same ones she saw back home before the raids, the fires, the smoke. On the horizon were the lights of Brooklyn, Staten Island, Manhattan and somewhere in the glow the Great Lady. Fatima leaned on a somewhat friend's shoulder. "If we see only this, the trip was worth it."

The other woman furled her lips and eyes as she relit a half cigarette she'd earned by way of a grabby kiss with a mechanic. "If I see only this, I want my goddamned money back."

chapter 3
TAMIKA

Courtyard of a Bronx West housing
project, Saturday, twenty-five days
before the hanging, 6:30 p.m. . . .

The Orange Houses were not orange. They were beaten
brick the color of the sky this drizzly dusk. Some long-
dead architect Casper Orange slapped together the nine
jail-like towers way back when. Small, deep-set windows
grayed cinderblock hallways noisy with need.

Mik hustled her grocery bags into tower #4 to beat the
rain. The elevator was grounded again. After a ten-flight
hike up the fire stairs she found NaNa passed out on the
couch. Tostitos Natural Blue crumbs buckshot the old
woman's chest. Nosebleed channel TV teased with an info-
mercial for an exercise machine nobody could afford. The
floor vibrated with the TV's fake enthusiasm jacked all

7

the way up. NaNa was not Deaf, but old-lady deaf. *Wha*jou say? *Wha*jou call me?

The woman had no folks, but everybody called her NaNa because she would sit your kid for a free meal. If you left a beer or two in the fridge for her, that was fine too. Going on three years now Mik and Mom didn't have the heart to tell the old gal she wasn't needed anymore.

Mik clicked to MTV to taunt herself. Some cutie was getting down with a guitar.

She put her hand on the TV speaker. Slow-strummed chords buzzed her fingertips and triggered a memory of Mom working that big body acoustic gathering closet dust the last ten years.

She clicked on her hearing aids. The music was ruined in them, the notes crackly edges and angles. Outside her window the city thumped with the coming night crowd: sellers, buyers, screamers, liars. In the background NaNa snored to cure comas.

Mik clicked off her aids.

This was what it was all about—the sadness muted. She could live and die without hearing another people-made noise. Except that guitar.

She changed the channel to the news. Closed captions flashed. HOUSE OVERRIDES PREZ'S VETO. CONTROVERSIAL IMMIGRATION BILL MOVES TO SENATE. BILL OFFERS REWARD $ TO ENCOURAGE REPORTING OF ILLEGALS.

Mik had enough problems without worrying about Mexicans stealing Americans' delivery bike jobs. She aimed the clicker, killed the TV and tucked a blanket around NaNa. Sure the old gal was asleep, Mik pecked a kiss onto that brow lined with seventy-some years of disappointment. She went to her room and pulled a throwaway briefcase from her closet. Inside were sketchbooks, pens and inks of all colors.

She kept the briefcase hidden behind her off-season threads. In her mind she heard Mom: *Why you spending all that time drawing instead of studying? You make all A's, you get yourself a free ride to college. You wanna end up like me, double shifting Target and Dunkin's? My daughter gonna end up slinging Hennessey cocktails at Applebee's for thug pimps, blah, blah, blah . . .*

Moms, Moms, Moms . . . How I want to love you.

Who wanted to go to college? After X463, aka Bronx-Orange high school, yo, Mik was *out*.

What then?

Whatever.

She studied her sketches. Cityscapes to the last one, they were remarkable, odd, the world a century after the plague. Buildings miraculously defied decay beneath gorgeous skies, no one around to enjoy them. Her streets were empty.

She checked her ink bottles. She was out of the most important color, the bones of every drawing, black. She tucked the briefcase into its hiding spot and crashed facedown into sheets that needed washing.

chapter 4
JIMMI

A Bronx West halfway house, Sunday,
twenty-four days before the hanging,
noon...

Jimmi Sixes the street poet eyed the bathroom mirror. He picked up the glitter lipstick the cross dresser down the hall left on the sink ledge. Over his cracked reflection he wrote:

WHY?

Jimmi's story: no Pops, his Moms a slave to the pipe. She put Jimmi in and out of foster care. With no prospects he signed on for what seemed a fair wage and adventure: the army. He left Bronx West for Basic without knowing he'd knocked up his girlfriend, the love of his life. He didn't find out she was getting heavy till he was overseas. He set the wedding for his next three-day leave. It never happened.

One morning a five-year-old with an IED strapped to her stomach skipped past Jimmi into the heart of a city market. The bomb malfunctioned. The half explosion tore the girl apart but didn't kill her instantly. Jimmi got to her on her third to last breath. As she died she asked him something in a language he didn't understand. The wounded man next to her coughed up, "She said, 'I know I am going into a coffin, but where will my face live?'"

PFC James Semprevivo sat in the smoking rubble and closed his eyes. He opened them nineteen days later to find out he was going home. He was eager to get back to the Bronx. His girl hadn't written him since a month before the suicide bomber. He left messages on her machine and her mother's, but neither woman called him back. Thirty feet into Bronx West he got the story. His gal lost the baby late term, then slit her wrists.

The VA set him up with a spot at the halfway house, a part-time sweep job at the hospital, benefit checks he forgot to cash and all the happy drugs he could stand. To those he added the occasional hit of crack cocaine. But now, eight months later, he was tired of being either jazzed or numb. He wrote on the mirror:

TIME TO FEEL AGAIN. KNOW THE TRIBE OF MAN FOR ALL ITS JOY AND HURT.

He dumped his many antipsychotic meds into the toilet, grabbed his oversized skateboard and poetry slam notebooks and did a swan dive out the second-story window.

A forward flip later he landed in a Dumpster soupy with wet cardboard and kitchen garbage. He was filthy but all right. He hopped his board and slalomed the back alley trash into the street and the thickening gray of the afternoon rain. "Hallelujah," he said, opening himself to the thunderstorm.

Jimmi Sixes was on a mission. He had to know: Was life worth living?

chapter 5
FATIMA

A noisy Bronx West side street, Monday,
twenty-three days before the hanging,
2:00 p.m. . . .

In Mexico they call the one who smuggles you into Texas the coyote, but the one who takes you from the refugee camps in Africa, across the ocean to New York, is the shark.

Fatima's shark sent her to a man who sold newspapers. He worked from a cluttered old house in what most considered a rough patch of Bronx. "You think this is rough?" Fatima said.

The man smiled. He had escaped a horrendous refugee situation a few years before. He was known to help illegals with connections to work and housing—for a price. "Do you have the money?"

Fatima gave the man half of what she had left after the boat ride: five hundred dollars.

The man counted the money. "Good. Be here by four a.m. to pick up your papers. After that I sell them to someone else." He scratched an address onto a paper scrap. "This woman will rent you a room for fifty dollars a week. Now sit, I have advice for you." All of it began with *Never,* ending with: "Never let the police see you. The laws are changing. In this neighborhood you are all right. The police do not come here much. They would have to arrest everyone if they did. Where I am sending you to sell your papers is also safe. You will work by the highway, just east of the Orange Houses. Many people shortcut to the subway there. If you work hard, you will save two hundred dollars each week. What will you do with all this cash?"

"In six months I will have enough to bring my sister here. Six months after that, we will bring two more."

"I believe you will. You are strong. Your English is excellent. You will make a good life here—if you keep your wits about you. Focus on but one thing: money. Keep to yourself." He gave her a newspaper. "Here. Learn about this crazy wonderful country. Do you have any questions?"

"How do I get to the Statue of Liberty?"

"Do not go there. It is a tourist trap."

Fatima paid four weeks rent to the old woman who showed her the small basement apartment. "I am sorry it is so bare and dark," the woman said.

"It is wonderful." Fatima meant what she said, always.

"On garbage days people on the nicer block just uphill

14

leave out treasures. Perhaps you will find some furniture. Where are your suitcases?"

Fatima tapped her backpack.

Her newspaper tucked under her arm, she explored her new neighborhood. She found a small park facing the veterans' hospital, whose buildings occupied much of the district's acreage. She sat at a concrete checkers table with a cup of cart coffee, the most wonderful she'd tasted, loaded with sugar. In the crisp clear afternoon air she wept.

A little girl approached. "Why are you crying?"

"Because I am happy."

"Then you got to be smiling. What happened to your face?" The girl pointed to a slash scar crossing Fatima's cheek.

Fatima smiled. "Sit. I must show you something." She waved to the girl's mother, watching from a distance. The mother waved back, gabbing into her phone. "Do you like angels?" Fatima asked the girl.

"Angels aren't real."

"Until you make one." Fatima pulled two sheets of newspaper from her daily and put one in front of the girl. "Do as I do." She folded the paper longwise, then in a series of crimps and tucks leading toward an angel.

The girl followed along. She eyed Fatima's left hand. "What happened to your fingers?"

Fatima smiled. Her pinky and ring finger were gone. If she held up the hand, say to block a machete blade, the angle of the slash through her palm would match that of the slash crossing her cheek. "You are a great angel maker." Fatima gave her own paper angel to the girl. "For your mother."

The girl ran off. "Ma, check it out."

Fatima started in on another angel.

"I saw what you did." Behind her was a tall, handsome young man, his skateboard tucked under his arm, his face a battered god's.

"Why are you crying?" Fatima said.

"Just mad happy is all," the man said.

"You are mad and happy at the same time?"

"Who's the third angel for?"

"I like always to have one in my pocket."

"For good luck."

"To give away." Fatima finished the angel with fast hands. She pulled a tab, and the angel collapsed. Another tab righted the angel, its wings a starburst. She gave it to the young man.

He studied it. He gently pressed it to his heart. "Yo, I'm Jimmi. Want you to meet a friend of mine. C'mon, just across the way there, the hoop courts."

Fatima studied the man, his smile, and knew he was a good man. She followed cautiously as this Jimmi led her across the street to the hospital yard.

"What's y'all's tag?" Jimmi said.

Fatima checked the side seam of her ratty sweatshirt. "Champion."

Jimmi's laugh was quiet and true. "Your name?"

"Fatima."

Veterans in wheelchairs played a ferocious game of basketball. Jimmi waved to the referee, a dour man.

Seeing Jimmi, the referee blew his whistle and barked, "Take five." He jogged to the chain-link fence. "Got a call from the halfway, James. Went AWOL, huh? I called your supe, dude said you missed work last two days."

"Been sick."

"Brother, are you jonesing?"

"Job brings me down, man. Was forcing myself over there when I met this young lady here."

"Where y'all holing up, James?"

"Fatima, George heads up volunteer activities for the hospital. George, Fatima is an artist."

George sighed. He turned from Jimmi to Fatima and sized her up with suspicious eyes. "Any teaching experience?"

Back in the refugee camp Fatima taught English to the younger girls. She lived to teach. She nodded.

"You looking for a job?" the sad George said.

Fatima squinted. "What are you paying?"

"Goodwill."

chapter 6
TAMIKA

A bodega, Tuesday, twenty-two days
before the hanging, 5:00 p.m. . . .

Mik helped out part-time after school. She was doing inventory when the matted, panicked German shepherd nipped at her jeans. She followed him to the next aisle, where old Joe Knows sat slumped on a flipped crate. He'd fallen asleep with a lit cigarette in his mouth again. Mik pinched the cigarette and helped the narcoleptic limp to the back office, where he slumped into a folding chair surrounded by cases of expired Goya cans.

Here's why he was Joe Knows: You come in feeling like trash, eyes and nose runny with flu, Joe says, "Under the weather?" You want to hot key your phone DUH, but instead you nod politely. Joe taps his temple, says, "See? Old Joe knows." He loved Mik, thought she should run for President of Everything. He paid her more than he had to, eight bucks an hour OTB. He knew Mik and Mom were saving for the surgery, the one Mik wasn't sure she wanted. She felt bad keeping Joe and Mom in the dark about her homework business money. But how else could she buy art supplies, paper, ink, that *pen*?

A flare outside the window itched Mik's eye. The magic man was cutting a curb rail on his double wide silver longboard. Jimmi Sixes did tricks on that plank to make a dull day gleam. He strode tall through the bodega door, put up his fist for a pound. "How you be, kid?" he said.

Mik winked.

A woman with a baby in her arms lugged a milk gallon to the counter. She hunted her purse for coins, didn't have enough. She grabbed the milk and started back for the fridge.

Jimmi stopped her with a five spot gently slapped to the counter. "On me."

"I couldn't," the woman said.

"How old your girl? She a girl, yeah?"

The woman nodded. "She about to make a year."

Jimmi bagged the milk for the woman and got the door for her.

"God bless you," the woman said.

"He does every day I'm aboveground," Jimmi said. "I reckon." He let the child squeeze his finger as the woman went. He nodded to Mik. "Think old Joe let you skip early?"

Key the phone: Y

"I'm-a hook you up with a friend of mine. Chick turns newspaper into seraphim."

Mik cocked her head, put up six fingers, mimed fluttering wings.

"Yup," Jimmi said. "Six-winged angels."

His board skated the gentle grade downhill in slow arcs, the front wheels parting the rainwater. They rode as one, Mik in front. He had his hands on her shoulders. She wished he would put them on her hips. He was eighteen, but dreaming was free.

Mik was crushing on near every boy these days, but Jimmi was different. He was so perfect she didn't want to sex it up with him. She wanted to skip straight to what she dreamed came after, the holding, staring into his sad black eyes.

Jimmi wasn't like that, though. He was big bro to her since she was a little kid. His lady, Alyssa was her name— no, Julyssa, was older than Jimmi before she killed herself. Jimmi always dated up and dated pretty, much prettier than flag-eared *Meek*-a Sykes.

He steered the board down a side street past an abandoned warehouse where the police used to keep impounded vehicles. The side of the building was forever fresh-tagged with hatred, Crip-Blood battles, the Latin Kings and MS-13. Four years back Jimmi pitched the precinct captain that he could round up kids to paint over the graffiti with scenes from the neighborhood. He would set the paint to rhyme. The captain loved it. Mik's contribution was the reservoir on a summer day, no people, no birds, just a clear lake reflecting empty sky—now buried after four years of taggers and bombers spanking the derelict garage. But one of Jimmi's lines still shouted out through the scrawl: LOVE KILLS TIME. From far away the letters seemed to come together from speckles of red and white paint, but when you got close you saw fist-sized hearts and clock faces with their hands stopped at midnight.

She heard him in her ear, a low, distant rumble, soothing but indecipherable. She clicked on her aids. "Say again," she said. She could talk a little in front of Jimmi. He never would make fun of anybody.

"You know the If trick?" Even her lousy aids couldn't ruin his deep, gentle voice.

She shook no.

"Learned it overseas. Think of a place you wanna go."

"Anywhere but here. Train ride."

"Okay, now put If in front of it, and y'all are there." He spoke slowly, enunciating each syllable, somehow managing not to sound patronizing. "Close y'all's eyes."

She did, trusting him to keep her from falling from the skateboard, letting him balance her, swaying with him, squeezing his hands.

"That's right, Mik. Now, If a train."

"If a train."

"See yourself standing on top of that train, girl. Let it get moving. You feel it now grooving? Clicka-clicka, wheels on tracks be soothing. Spread your wings, catch the wind of kings, lift yourself to the heart of things, swing moons and stars and galactic rings."

She almost saw it: Tamika Sykes standing on a train, stepping onto a cloud, reaching up . . .

"Open your eyes, kid."

The board stopped. They were by the highway overpass. In front of Mik and between a mound of garbage and a torched car was a stack of newspapers on an upturned milk crate. Behind the stack was a tall beautiful girl, her head wrapped in a shawl. She wore a curious smile. A scar on her cheek peeked out from the head-wrap. Her eyes were big and light brown against her dark skin. She wore a dirty hand-me-down coat too small for her, threadbare jeans and hole-shot sneakers. Despite the cold, damp day she wore no socks.

Jimmi took the girl's hand and brought it to Mik's.

The girl's hand was rough like the sackcloth the root vegetables came in on delivery day at Joe Knows's place. Her fingers were warm, strong.

Confused, the women turned to Jimmi.

Jimmi nodded. "Here's what I see: two artists. Y'all are gonna create the most beautiful thing in the world."

And what's that? Mik thought as her phone vibrated. She drew back her hand to pull the phone from her pocket. Caller ID said MOM, who always texted, never called. Mik turned away, cupped her hand to hide her voice as she said, "Yeah?"

Mom was screaming, her words wicked static in the cheap phone. Mik crushed the receiver to her ear, still couldn't put together what Mom was saying. Panicked, she hit speaker, yelled, "You okay? Where are you?"

"*RIGHT BEHIND YOU,*" blasted from the phone. "*I SAID, Y'ALL GET AWAY FROM THAT CRAZY JIMMI. CRACKHEAD GONNA—*"

22

Mik snapped the phone, spotted Mom running along the Target sidewalk toward her.

Jimmi made double peace signs, one for Mik, one for the paper girl, and sailed off on his board, no rush. "Don't sweat yourself, kid. Mind y'all's Moms."

The paper girl stepped back, putting the stack of news between herself and trouble. She stared at Mik.

Mom spun Mik with a shoulder grab. "How many times I got to tell you, Mika? Y'all know how them vets are, coming back all whacked and jacked on drugs. Look at that poor boy. He got the itch all right. You don't know what they're liable to do, child. Just because he sick don't mean you got to share his ills." Mom eyed the newspaper girl. "What happened to the little old Mexican man used to work this spot?"

The girl gulped.

Mom spun for the O Houses, shouting something.

Mik couldn't make out the words in the wind playing hell with her aids. She signed, WHAT?

Mom signed back stiffly, I SAID GET OVER HERE, NOW.

Mik signed, YOU DON'T HAVE TO GET ALL FREAKED OUT. RELAX.

Mom, coming back for Mik now: "I caught about half of that."

The paper girl tucked a note into Mik's hand.

Mom grabbed Mik's arm. "Mika, come."

Girls on the corner laughed at Mik as Mom towed her home. Two boys eyed Mom, early thirties and eye candy, even in her Target uniform. One boy put a peace sign to his lips, his tongue between his fingers. The other hollered, "Yo baby, my boy lick y'all's—"

Mik clicked off her aids. The boys' howling hushed. Mom's anger could not reach her. The nastiness evaporated.

Everything.

Just.

Faded away.

Taking shelter in the near silence, Mik looked back at the papergirl. She was waving. No, she was signing, HELLO, GOOD-BYE, I LOVE YOU.

I *love* you?

Mik looked down at what the girl tucked into her hand: a paper angel with six wings.

Mom jerked Mik forward. The angel fell from Mik's palm into the rain stream washing toward the sewer.

"Mika, I'm sorry. What else do you want me to say?" Mom popped a Relpax.

NaNa stroked Mom's hand. "Sandrine, my hairdresser, she got the migraines too, she goes to the acupuncture, headache gone, girl."

"My junk insurance doesn't cover the acupuncture, sweetheart." Then to Mik: "You hear what I'm telling you, right? I know it isn't Jimmi's fault, but he is what he has become, dig? Are your aids on? Turn, them, *on. Now.* Those boys see things over there . . . I don't know. Crazy Jimmi Sixes means himself every flavor of harm. You don't want to be there when he snaps."

Mik spooned chili onto three plates. "He's nice to me."

"The devil's sugar will rot your soul," Mom said.

"Now-now, Drine Sykes, I wouldn't pin the devil on Jimmi," NaNa said. "Confusion yes, Satan no. I sat that child how many nights when he wasn't in foster care, his poor mother scrambling all over God's world. Jimmi is sweet and he is good."

Mom rolled her eyes.

Mik signed, WE OWE THAT PAPER GAL AN APOLOGY.

Mom massaged her left eye. "I don't know what she said," she said to NaNa.

"Speak, child," NaNa said.

Mik cleared her throat. "I think we should have that newspaper girl over for dinner."

Mom squinted, cocked her head.

Mik avoided Mom's look. Exactly why was she drawn to this paper girl? *Must be something in her eyes. Something nobody else has.* That newspaper angel was pretty hype too. More than that, the chick signed, but she wasn't deaf. Her hands were slower and clumsier than Mom's even. Mom was mediocre on a good day despite Mik's constant teaching. Why would the girl know hand language?

"Imagine that." NaNa picked her teeth with a postcard from the junk mail left out on the kitchen table. "I do believe at long last Mika's getting lonesome."

"Tt, chili's getting cold," Mik said.

chapter 7
FATIMA

A diner, Tuesday, twenty-two days
before the hanging, 8:00 p.m. . . .

The food was inexpensive and delicious. Fatima savored each french fry as she wrote her sister a letter that ended with *Good-bye, I love you—*

—HELLO, GOOD-BYE, I LOVE YOU. This was all the sign she knew. What had passed between Jimmi's friend and Fatima as they shook hands? Something intense and immediate. Something—

"Something else?" the waitress said.

"Please tell me how to get to the Statue of Liberty."

"Serious?" She called to the other waitress, "Carmen, how you get to the Statcha Lib'dy?"

"Never been. I think you got to take a boat."

Shouting from behind the counter. Two men who had been sitting at the next table escorted a handcuffed dishwasher from the kitchen. They seemed tired, distressed, not as distressed and tired as the dishwasher begging, "Por favor, tengo dinero. Te pagaré. Te pagaré."

The waitress said, "No te preocupes, Guillermo. No llores."

The other waitress, Carmen, whispered, "They prob'ly shut us down now."

"What happened?" Fatima said.

"Immigration police."

Fatima fought the urge to hide her face in her shawl. "May I have my bill?"

chapter 8
JIMMI

The train tracks, Wednesday, twenty-
one days before the hanging, just past
midnight . . .

Jimmi weaved in and out of the trackside trash. He wanted to rip away his skin. Was this physical withdrawal or his spirit's hunger? A knock of crack would help him get through to tomorrow—

Don't.

He was low on money, but he wasn't going back to the house to pick up his VA check before he beat the pill habit. If he could outlast the gnawing another week or so, he could go back fresh and tell the doctors he was done with the drugs, the therapy, the halfway situation. He would insist he was moving on into the Full Now: a good clean job that supported a family he would never let down.

But not yet. He needed time away from all the old routines and places, the sad faces. Some alone time would clear his mind enough to keep him sober. The thought of going back to his part-time janitor gig at that depressing hospital made him queasy.

"Soup," he said to no one. "Get some heat into you."

The elevated highway straddled the tracks. Jimmi pushed a rotting 4 x 8 plywood sheet from a cut in the track wall. At the tunnel's mouth was a wheeled garbage cart nearly filled with supplies, scavenged canned food, plastic tarps, and a car battery mounted with a flashlight. He pushed through the dark, a left here, two rights, another left. He knew the maze by heart. This was his hideout since childhood. He came to what had been the start of a subway station eighty years ago. He got the butane hotplate going, pocked a soup can with his knife and dropped it onto the heat. In the flame's light he swept sand from a patch of floor with his coat. He chalked the concrete so:

WHY DO ANGELS FLY TOWARD LIGHTNING?
THEY THINK THEY'LL SURVIVE IT?
TRULY FRIGHTENING.
SWOOP IN FAST AND GRAB THE WONDER.
GET OUT FASTER. BEAT THE THUNDER.
THEY LISTEN. GLISTEN. MAGIC EACH DAY.
MAYBE. PLEASE. TO SHOW US THE WAY?

But what those girls could make together. With their gifts, they had a responsibility to do it, to create the beauty that went past paper and pen and sculpture and into the

29

vibe. You can't describe it except to call it something like hope. He prayed Mik and Fatima would hook up until he remembered he was too mad at God to ask for anything.

Now he saw the other girl, the child suicide bomber, legless, bleeding out in front of him on the sandy subway platform. He closed his eyes but still saw her, would always see her. Why didn't he grab her as she skipped past him? Could he have stopped her from detonating that IED? What would have happened if he never signed on for overseas action, if he stayed home to be with his lady? Would he have saved his baby that night? Saved Julyssa?

He stared at his fingers, the ones that had focused a rifle sight, cocked the hammer, snapped the trigger, pulled grenade pins. He wondered if his goddam filthy hands were good for anything but ruin.

He lifted the soup can by its lip from the stove. The metal ring burned his fingers as he set it aside. He didn't care. He kept his hand on that ring until he couldn't tell if the metal was hot anymore. He turned off the stove and trembled himself into a sweaty sleep.

chapter 9
TAMIKA

Mik's bedroom, Wednesday, twenty-one days before the hanging, 1:30 a.m. . . .

She set aside her sketch and thought *If a city sky . . .*

She pictured herself soaring over the Bronx, clouds vaporizing, the sky empty but for the bright blue in it. She felt good for a while, then cold as she flew higher. The sky turned cobalt. Pulling her robe around her, she drifted into sleep.

She woke in a panic to stop a dream about a six-winged paper doll catching fire in a bomb-burned sky.

She had fallen asleep at her desk, her face greasy with night sweat. The window was open, the room damp. The only light was a dim red from her clock radio, 4:04 a.m. Her desk lamp had blown out. She was sure something evil was in the room.

She went to Mom's room. Mom was crashed out on the bed facedown, her pants on the floor. She'd conked in her Dunkin' shirt. The room smelled sad, like stale donuts.

Mik wanted to cuddle her, almost did, didn't.

She went to the main room, sank into the couch and clicked the TV to snow for the soft purple light in it. A trace of NaNa lingered in the couch cushions—street vendor perfume.

"Saw you scrambling this morning," Mom said. "Finish that homework?"

"Yeah," Mik said. It was somebody else's.

"Are your aids turned on, or are you trapped in slow motion?"

"Nice brooch."

"Sarcasm isn't pretty on you." Mom fussed with her hair in the hallway mirror.

WHY YOU GET DRESSED SO NICE TO WORK WHERE NOBODY APPRECIATES YOU? Mik signed.

"What?"

"I said, you look pretty, Ma." Mik grabbed her bag and went.

From behind battered card tables, street hawkers begged folks to buy fruit, shish kebob, trinkets and, at the end of the block, newspapers.

The paper girl smiled when she saw Mik.

Possible causes for the scar on the girl's cheek flashed Mik's mind: a switchblade, ringed fingers curled into a fist.

She put fifty cents into the girl's sooty hand, wanted to ask her over for dinner, but the words wouldn't come.

HELLO, the girl signed.

Mik nodded. She wanted to ask the girl how she knew sign, but that would require a whachamacallit, conversation. "Nice day," she said and signed as she hurried away.

Mik picked a back row spot to nap through English. She dozed with her chin propped in her hands. Her face slipped through her fingers. Her head whacked the desk. Blood dripped from her nose.

Pounding on the floor, the desks, all eyes wild, howling mouths—

Click. Aids off. Everybody a mile away.

She read Rodriguez's lips as the old woman led her to the nurse's office. "Mika, is that alcohol on your breath?"

"Cough medicine," Mik coughed.

Speech therapy: The old hippie teacher smelled like licorice and Certs, total pot cover. After, out in the hall girls flocked around a new boy. Mik clicked on her hearing aids.

"What's y'all's name?" said Shanelle, the girl fresh from juvie.

He wore his hair in dreads beaded Day-Glo orange, green, yellow. He licked his lips. "Jaekwon."

Shanelle said, "Where y'all from?"

The bell went off—a slasher movie scream in Mik's hearing aids. Kids scattered.

"And where y'all going?" The boy grabbed Shanelle's hand to hold her back from running off to class.

Mik hurried past. Shanelle backed up hard, knocked Mik off her feet, her books spreading out over the buffed floor.

"Fat bitch," Shanelle said. "Watch where you going."

"You watch where *you* going," Mik said.

Shanelle crossed her eyes, exaggerated Mik's words with a thick tongue, "Ooh wah whay *ooh* gah-in."

The Jaekwon cat helped Mik pick up her books. He was checking out her butt, Mik noticed.

Sha's eyes narrowed. She pulled her sweatshirt zipper down to show some serious cleavage. "Jae-baby, lemme give y'all my numbuh."

The bucktooth G pimp-limped up to Mik, helped her with her books. "What up, girl?"

"Easy, son," this Jaekwon said. "I got it."

Little G was nerd cute, but Jaekwon was seriously bangin'. That he would spend a look on Mik blew her mind. He was a total player—all that lip-licking, his cheeks sucked in like one of those no-shirt cats on the cover of the romance novels at Target. She almost laughed. He winked at her.

Shanelle flipped off Mik as a teacher clapped them to class.

The rain came down hard as she jumped onto the bus. Jimmi Sixes swung past on his skateboard. He skid-stopped at the ninety-nine cents store, under the awning covering the outdoor bins. From one of them he pulled a pack of colored construction paper. His clothes were soaked, rumpled. He was pale.

34

She made change for a dude who needed laundry quarters and got back to doodling another empty cityscape.

Joe Knows watched her from the customer side of the counter, said something.

She clicked on her aids. "Sorry Joe?"

"How long before you and Mom have enough saved up for the implant?"

"Long time."

Joe nodded. "I been thinking about this. I been on that Internet thing, looking up the operation. I wanna pay for it."

Mik squinted.

"You're a great kid. I wanna see you do good. It was either the surgery or art school, but I figure you're gonna get a scholarship."

She hadn't planned on having to decide about the operation for another four or five years. She squeezed Joe's hand, shook no. She keyed her phone: BUT THANX

"Mik, what am I gonna spend it on? I got no midgets, no mortgage. C'mon. Talk to your mom about it. Will you?"

Shanelle whittled a stick with her box cutter while her posse tagged the handball wall with silver perma-markers. Mik pretended not to see them as she hurried past.

"Yo Dumbo," Sha said. "Y'all best stay away from that Jaekwon. Serious. Deaf bitch. Yo, you hear me?"

Mik heard her. She kept those aids on when near danger zones like busy streets and handball courts filled with psycho chicks. She tried not to walk away too fast, pretending she wanted to go shopping instead of home. No way was she crossing Sha's path, not with her posse sharing brown-bag forties and smoking blunts.

Mik went to the paper girl's spot. The girl wasn't there. Done for the day, she was towing her empty crates uphill by way of a beat-up rack duct-taped to a wobbly skateboard. She had a few leftover papers under her arm. Mik hurried after her into the wildwood park but lost her in the path's twisting. She came to a fork and picked the wrong trail. She doubled back and found the girl far ahead, hurrying out of the park. The girl covered ground fast with those long legs. She had to stand close to six feet.

Mik called after the girl but not loud enough, chased uphill, swore to take up exercise as she sucked wind. Weed stalks spiked rubble in abandoned lots. In the fading light a methamphetamine pipe blinked. The girl disappeared around the corner of a crumbling row house, the buildings on either side boarded up and swamped with dying pest trees.

Mik found herself in an alley that opened onto a yard of cracked cement painted pink, a bright spot in the gray. A mangy old cat hunkered by the cellar door. It limped away into the weeds at the sight of Mik. She knocked, and the door opened on the first hit. Inside the small basement studio were a card table and on the floor a mattress made neatly with a red blanket. A short stack of newspapers squared perfectly against the wall. Pinned to the walls, doing handstands on the lone sill were tiny paper figurines, birds, angels, ballerinas, a soccer player upside down in a bicycle kick. All were painted with bin nail polish, sparkly black, neon red, Day-Glo green, dark blue, mystical brown glitter.

"My friend," the girl said. She'd come from the bathroom door now swinging shut on its spring. "Do you make a habit of breaking into people's rooms?"

Mik gulped. "How do I get home from here?"

"That depends on where you live."

"Can you walk me?"

"Bombs deafened some of the children back home," Fatima said as she and Mik walked the back way along the tracks. "My sister and I watched the woman from the UN teach them sign, but only for one day before a raid split the camps. Perhaps someday when the fighting ends I will return home. For now I am so lucky to live in these beautiful United States." Fatima stepped over a rat skipping out of the garbage. "Do you know McDonald's restaurant?"

Mik smiled.

"His fried apple cake, the fritter? Magic. Once you bite into it, all problems disappear. May I treat you?"

"Gotta get home." The O Houses were just downhill. Mik scanned the street for Shanelle, not in sight.

"I hope I see you again."

"Come up for dinner." She hadn't talked this much to a stranger since she was five. What was it about this paper girl that suddenly had Mik feeling comfortable enough to initiate not just conversation but an invitation to dinner?

"Perhaps you should ask your mother first. I will go buy cake for dessert. What is your room number?"

"My apartment number?"

"You live in an *apartment*?"

chapter 10
FATIMA

The Orange Houses, Wednesday, twenty-one days before the hanging,
7:00 p.m. . . .

The elevator surprised Fatima with its great speed. Electricity was everywhere in this enormous building, even in the hallways. The floors and walls were strong stone. Mik and her family were wealthy. Fatima's tattered clothes and sneakers and the cheap fritters she purchased half price shamed her. A chubby old woman huffed toward Mik's door from the other end of the hall. Fatima nodded.

The woman was mistrustful. "Yes?"

"I am a friend of Mik. I think."

The woman eyed Fatima's shawl, opened the door and yelled in, "Y'all expecting a six-foot Muslim gal?"

"But where's your mother?" Mik's mom said.

Fatima pointed to her heart.

Mom shook her head. "Child," she said.

"Oh child." The kindly NaNa took Fatima's hand.

"Fatima, sixteen, living alone?" Mom said. "That won't do."

"I'm-a ask around the church for a place for her." NaNa popped the rest of her fritter into her mouth as she studied Fatima. "Lovely headdress. What's that like, being Islamic?"

"I am not Muslim."

"You're not Christian."

"No."

"Then daggit, what are y'all?"

"I am human."

NaNa thought about that. "I guess that's all right. What's the scarf for?"

"To keep my head warm."

"Worse goes worst, you come stay with me. I got enough room up there for a *village* of Muslims."

"Thank you, but I must remain uphill. I am safest there." These Americans were wonderful people. She was hesitant at first to answer their questions, to accept Mik's invitation. But now she was glad she came. Back in the camps she told herself she would be fine on her own, but now she knew she had been lying to herself. She missed her sister.

Mik had been watching her. She broke from the table to clear the dinner plates. Fatima helped. After, they went to Mik's room. Mik showed her a sketch.

Fatima ran her fingers over the dried ink. She caught

a tear with a cupped hand to stop it from splattering the empty cityscape.

"That bad?" Mik said.

"Beyond wonderful, but your streets, where are your people?"

Mik yanked the sketchbook away and hid it under her pillow as Mom came in with clothes and sneakers. "Try these on, girlfriend," she said. "I can let down the pants."

Fatima took in the embroidered jeans, the plush sweatshirts, a leather jacket broken in just right. The sneakers were big on her, but so luxurious with their padding.

"Thank you, Mom."

"You look adorable," Mom said.

Mik fiddled with her hearing aids.

chapter 11
JIMMI

The cave, Thursday, twenty days before
the hanging, 3:00 a.m. . . .

Jimmi Sixes folded the colored construction paper into tiny shapes.

"Night patrol," he whispered. "Night vision goggles. They call it night vision, civilians without sin, grenaded to ruin, collateral mayhem, won't happen say them, green blur and wasteland."

He flashed back to the desert and his armored tank rolling over towns held together by mortar thinned with dust and husk, everything ancient, so durable and fragile at the same time.

He regretted he'd dumped all those antipsychotic drugs down the halfway house toilet.

He fed cracker bits to the rats. "Food," he whispered.

He went where he'd been going since he was a kid whenever he was hungry and out of money. He went to Joe Knows.

He waited in front of the locked roll gate. Joe and his old dog Tranquilito limped uphill with the sunrise, like always.

Joe stopped at the sight of Jimmi. He threw an arm over Jimmi's shoulder. "Ah kid," Joe said. "Joe knows. Joe knows, son."

"Joe, was it like this for you, when you came back from your war? Was it this bad?"

Joe made Jimmi breakfast. He smoked his Camel deep into the filter, his lids heavy as he watched Jimmi eat, though Jimmi didn't eat much.

"Jimmi, you gotta let me take you back to the hospital, son."

"Can't go back there, Joe."

"Lemme get that coffee hot."

When Joe turned to refill Jimmi's cup, Jimmi slipped away.

chapter 12
TAMIKA

The Sykeses' apartment, Thursday,
twenty days before the hanging,
6:00 a.m....

She woke with an ear infection. This happened once a
month. She was used to the pain. She went through the
drill: scrub the ears and aids with hot soapy water, then
peroxide, then coat them with Neosporin. She popped the
first of the ten generic antibiotic tablets that were always
on hand, always liable to upset her stomach.

On her way to school she stopped for a daily. Fatima
wouldn't let her pay. She gave her a paper angel painted
violet. "When will I see you again?" Fatima said.

"Have to work this afternoon. Dinner tomorrow?"

"My house this time."

Mik was supposed to notify the principal's office when the speech therapist didn't show. She didn't. She unfolded and refolded Fatima's paper angel. By the time the class was close to ending, she knew how to make the angel from fresh paper.

She hated when folks felt sorry for her, but she liked to feel sorry for other folks. She wasn't sure why. Being sixteen without a Moms? Scary. The bell stabbed her ears.

She ducked into the bathroom, took out her aids and pressed her ears to the sides of her head. If God was real, someday he, she, whatever would answer her prayer and her ears would stay down when she took away her hands.

Today was not the day.

She rolled out Mom's bunched braids and ponied her loops low to tie back her ears. Her hair was kinked, maybe even pretty.

The new boy Jaekwon was in her art class. Punk. "Then why y'all sweating the hairstyle?" she asked the bathroom mirror.

She got to art early and sat by the window. The Jaekwon dude just had to torture her by sitting across from her. The assignment was to sketch each other. She surprised herself by getting him dead-on except for his eyes, which she left blank like those in a Greco Roman bust.

He drew her with footballs for breasts.

She tried to think of anything but knocking boots with him.

"So you death, huh?" he said to her chest.

She imagined kissing his lips as she read them. She cleared her throat. "Death?"

Jaekwon tapped his ears. "You kind of can't tell. Like, you talk good. Like, not like a mental I mean."

"Um, like thank you." She wondered if he was lying about her voice. Did she really sound okay?

"Yo, you got a nice body."

She frowned as she felt his sneaker tap hers under the table. "Y'all best get back to your drawing," she said.

Tap on her shoulder: security guard chick, hand out, palm up, Mik's hearing aids. "Left these in the bathroom again, Mika."

Mik forced herself to smile thanks, tucked the aids into her pocket, buried her face in her sketchpad.

Jae tapped her hand. "Do it hurt? Straining to hear and all?"

She studied his eyes undressing the girl at the end of the table now. "No," she said. "It doesn't hurt."

She pressed her palm to her ear. Damned infection left her feeling as if an angry carpenter were driving at her head with a nail gun.

At lunch the janitor was painting Mik's stairwell spot to cover the scratchiti that still showed through: LATIN KINGS RULE, BLOODS SUCK. The paint stink dizzied her. She grabbed a bench in the cafeteria. From the far corner she watched Shanelle nuzzle Jaekwon.

Mik dumped the usual gluey PBJ and a past ripe apple out of her brown bag. The same old note from NaNa said: HAVE A BLESSED DAY ☺

46

The G swung up to her table. "Yo, how's my shorty?" He tripped as he sat.

Mik hurt for him. She keyed her phone: LETZ SEE IT.

The G took out his homework, frowned at somebody behind Mik.

Jaekwon plunked next to her, grabbed her sandwich, bit in. He leaned close to her, his eyes too pretty, cruel.

Shanelle and her crew came over. Jae's boys followed. Folks crowded around the table, lots of talking, whispering, hissing in Mik's aids, too much going on, sensory overload.

Shanelle gave Mik slit eyes as she slid into Jaekwon's lap.

Jae told everybody, "This chick can *draw*. She *mad* good."

Sha grabbed Jae's arm. "Jae, you come over my house, I show you my drums. Play you my set, private concert style, na-mean?"

"Chicks don't play drums, girl, c'mawn."

Shanelle finger popped in Jae's face. "I so *do*. Teacher said I got skills. Gonna be mad famous someday. How 'bout you, *Meek-a*? You play mu-sic?" Sha exaggerated her mouth and eye movements. She turned to Jae, showed him her fingers, calluses thick from hand drumming. "Check 'em out. I'm a wild woman on the slaps. Touch them tips. Feel how hard they are? Them's musician's scars, baby."

"You probably burned them on your curling iron." Did she actually speak that thought? She was *so* dead.

47

Laughing, screaming came from mouths stretched in long ovals. Girls snapped fingers. Boys pounded the table, *bock, bock, bock!*

The concussions blew out Mik's aids in half-second pulses, but she didn't dare turn them off—not with Sha's brows angled down, her lips trembling.

"She just *read* you, Shanelle," some chick said. "She read you from here to filth."

Jaekwon laughed, "Dag. *Dag.*"

Mik scanned the cafeteria for The G, lost in the crowd.

Hard fingers grabbed her chin to turn her head.

"Ey!" Sha said. "Ey, Mika, you readin' my lips *now*, you elephant-eared bitch?"

That got everybody *ooh*-ing. Kids circled to watch the coming brawl.

Mik left.

Shanelle followed. She gave Mik a flatsy, kicked away Mik's sneaker, snapped Mik's ear.

Mik swung first but Shanelle swung harder and decked Mik. The girls rolled over the floor in a vicious smack fight. The G got in there to try to break it up and caught a Sha slap that made his head wobble. He slumped to his knees.

Mik glimpsed Jaekwon grinning with his boys. "I ain't gettin' in on that," he said, something like that, hard to tell with all the noise polluting Mik's junky hearing aids. "*You* bust it up."

Mik put herself between Shanelle and The G, took another shot from Sha as she protected the kid.

A few seconds later the lunch ladies had Sha in arm locks.

A tug at Mik's cuff.

The dazed G was on the floor. Shanelle's handprint was a bright sting on his cheek. His bloody lip stuck to his braces. "Sorry."

"Sorry?" Mik said. Her ear throbbed where Sha smacked it. She helped The G to his feet. He was near tears as everyone laughed at him.

Over his shoulder Jaekwon was smiling. "How I do love a cat fight," he said.

"Just hear me out," the principal said. "Shanelle will be suspended. A police report will be filed."

Mik keyed her phone: NO RPRT

"You don't have to file charges, Tamika, but I have to file a statement." The principal frowned. "Look, I know it's not easy for you here—"

"She can handle it," Mom said.

"Mrs. Sykes, as I believe I told you, we have options. The special programs school where Tamika can be with kids who—"

"As I believe I told *you*, sir, regular school is just fine for my daughter. Right, Mika?"

Mik marched out of school into the bright cold day, peeled off as she signed, I'M LATE FOR JOE'S.

Mom followed Mik uphill. "So am I."

Mik stopped. HE CALLED YOU?

"How come you didn't tell me, Mika? The man is offering you a chance at a normal life."

"*Nor*mal."

"Wait up. I don't want you walking alone from school

anymore. That Shanelle don't play. I saw what she did to that girl last year, that buck fifty down the side of her jaw. Y'all have that Fatima pick you up from now . . . " Mom looked up as an orange dragonfly floated past her. She jumped back as another—purple—landed on her shoulder.

Mik caught a third, bright red. Not bugs but paper, folded.

"Lord," Mom said. "It's snowing colors."

Tiny angels pirouetted from the sky. Ballerinas, ballplayers, birds. On a hawk's wings was written PEACE. Mik looked for Fatima. She found Jimmi standing on a mailbox. He was releasing hundreds of paper dolls into the breeze.

Shoppers young and old scrambled for the dolls. Everyone was laughing.

Mik grinned.

Jimmi slid down the mailbox and headed for Mik with a rainbow painted angel.

Mom cut him off. "Will you please leave the child alone, James? Please now, before I call the police."

Jimmi bowed his head, tucked the angel into the lapel of Mom's overcoat, stepped onto his skateboard and drifted downhill. His jeans hung loose on him, his shirt baggy, his face gaunt.

Mik marched past Mom with DO YOU HAVE TO HATE HIM SO MUCH, MA?

"Slow down with those hands. I can't understand—"

"I know you can't." She clicked off her aids and slumped toward Joe Knows's joint.

" . . . account number already set up in your name, Sandrine, in trust for Mik. All y'all have to do is type in the . . . " Joe fell asleep.

Mik stopped petting the German shepherd to tap Joe's fingers, yellowed and bent from sixty years of smoking.

Joe picked up where he left off: " . . . password, go to online bill paying, cut a check to the doc, hospital, whatever. I think there's enough cash to cover everything."

Mom hugged him.

"Hey now." Joe patted Mom's back. "This is no big deal, okay? It's just life. And you, my friend." He winked at Mik.

Mik winked back.

"You're thinking, maybe I don't want to get the operation." He tapped his temple. "Joe knows. Look, take your time. The money's yours for whatever. I know you'll do something beautiful with it."

That night Mik hit Mom's closet and dug out the old guitar. She opened the window to let in the wind. Straddling the sill, she turned her aids on and all the way up. She plucked the low string, her cheek on the guitar's belly. The vibrations reached deep into her head. She plucked harder, the bass note pulsing in her stomach . . .

Plucked harder, fuzzy fingers walking her spine . . .

Pluck—

The string snapped, the cut-off sound cold and sharp in Mik's ears.

A poke at her shoulder.

Mom was home two hours early, a dark brown starburst on her chest as if she'd been shot.

"What the—"

"Coolatta machine exploded. Running a stupid summer shake these fall days." She grabbed the guitar. "How'd you like if I poked through your closet?" She dug a string out of the case, threaded the fresh E through the bridge.

"Play for me," Mik said. "I'll rest my hands on the belly."

"I'm sure I forget how." Mom frowned, picked at a chip in the worn fret board. "You gonna get the operation?"

Mik looked down into the courtyard. Drunk dudes swore at each other to wake the world. She wanted to click off her aids but didn't dare while Mom was in this state, ready to cry or scream or both. "Ma, if you never gonna play that guitar again, why you restringing it?"

Drine Sykes shoved the guitar into her closet and grabbed a fresh shirt. "I gotta get back to work."

chapter 13
FATIMA

The Veterans Administration hospital,
Friday, nineteen days before the
hanging, 3:00 p.m. . . .

Word was getting out about Fatima's teaching. Yesterday she had two students. Today the ten chairs around the rec room table were full. Most of the students were young children taking time off from visiting their parents upstairs. One of the latecomers was a burn patient covered in bandages. A girl gasped when the man came to the table in his motorized wheelchair.

"Sorry," the man said. He turned for the door.

Fatima brought him back to the table and sat him next to the shocked girl. Seeing Fatima at ease with the man calmed the girl. "Now," Fatima said, "today we are going to make a school of newsprint dolphins."

She rushed from the hospital to pick up Mik from school. Mik was out front, her eyes darting about the street for the bully girl.

"I thought she has been suspended," Fatima said.

"Doesn't mean she isn't waiting for us," Mik said. "You're lucky you don't have to go to school."

"I am finding many wonderful books in the garbage on the other side of the reservoir, outside the college."

At the supermarket Fatima said, "This is ridiculous, all of the things we can buy here."

"This store is booty. You should see the rich folks' markets downtown."

"Five kinds of apples?"

"Apples are lame."

"We can only dream of apples where I come from. What is this, this star fruit? This is food to make our imaginations strong." Fatima gathered up an armload.

They sat on milk crates in Fatima's yard, eating what they cooked on a grill they found on the street. The arthritic cat crawled out from the woods into Fatima's lap. She fed him bits of fish. "I call him Every Third because he comes only every third day. He is a stray, but he lingers longer with each visit. With winter near he is realizing he needs a friend." She said to the cat, "Do not fear, little one. My door is always open to you. How would I say this in sign?"

"Why you want to know?"

"For when I return to my country. To teach the children. Show me."

Mik showed her. Fatima was a quick study.

Mik indicated the cinderblock fence. "Weren't these walls pink?" She signed as she spoke.

"I changed the color yesterday to amuse myself. Next week they will be turquoise." The twilight sun on the freshly painted orange walls warmed Fatima. She took in the backyard: swept clean cement, plastic vines hanging from a sawed-down willow trunk, a bowl chopped into the top for a birdbath. "By springtime we will have an oasis back here for my sister's arrival." She hoped Mik would not ask if any word had arrived from the camps.

She didn't. She said, "We should paint the walls a rainbow."

"I know where we can get the paint. Come. In that lot back there, through all that creeping thorn, is a treasure palace."

Dead vines covered the house. Its windows had been smashed long ago. Gauzy bits of curtain twisted in the breeze. In the shed were enough paint buckets to cover the house. "Lots of light green here," Mik said. "Cool color."

"This is the Statue of Liberty's color, no?"

"Never been. Hey, the dolls, why not pipe cleaners or wood or clay? Why always newspaper?"

"It was all we had." They pushed through the weeds choking the lot, into the abandoned house.

"You scared?" Mik said.

"It would be no fun otherwise, Sister Mik."

Graffiti covered the walls and ceilings. The staircase was carved with initials and years that went back to the 1970s. In the kitchen Fatima found a cracked clock radio and a dusty cat box. In the home office were looted medical cabinets and books that illustrated procedures for surgeries, polyp removal, abortion. Mik eyed the surgery chair. "Let's get out of here."

A weed tree grew through the roof. This high uphill one could see across the valley, west to the Riverdale cliffs. Below, the Orange Houses were an ocean of lights. Up here the streetlights didn't work. Fatima and Mik pointed out shooting stars to each other.

"Should I get the operation?" Mik said.

Fatima eyed the moon. "Only you can say. Operation or not, you must get your mother to teach you to play guitar."

"How did your mother die?"

"We were out collecting fire sticks on a night like this, Mom, my sister and I. We saw torch lights, how do you say it here, flashlights. The men were coming. I was small, my sister smaller, we would not have made it back to camp. My mother told us to run. We did but turned back when we saw Mom was not running with us. Mom said, 'This is nothing, what will happen next. This is nothing. Go. Go and be strong. Be happy always.' She pushed us on and remained behind and ran in the opposite direction so the men would chase her and lose track of us. That was the last we saw of her." Fatima clapped her hand on

Mik's shoulder. "Jimmi taught you his If game, yes?" She closed her eyes, said, "If a bright future. Do you see it?"

"Tell me."

"You, my sister, and I are in Liberty's torch." She opened her eyes. "Look at these stars. I cannot believe that I am here, that you are here. This is all we need." Fatima pointed to the highest point in the sky. "Do you see her? My mother. She is happy. Do you see her winking at us?" Fatima signed to the sky, HELLO, GOOD-BYE, I LOVE YOU.

chapter 14
TAMIKA

Mik's bedroom, Saturday, eighteen days
before the hanging, 2:00 a.m. . . .

Mik couldn't sleep. She went into Mom's room and lay next
to her. Mom woke, rubbed her eyes, yawned in the gray
green streetlight flickering through the curtain. "What's
wrong?"

Mik stared into her mother's eyes, held her hand.

"Mika?"

"Shhhhh. Let's just stay like this."

chapter 15
JIMMI

The cave, Saturday, eighteen days
before the hanging, 2:30 a.m. . . .

Jimmi heated the tip of a ballpoint with his lighter.
He stripped off his socks and burned small blue 6s into
the secret places, the bottom of his feet, between his toes.
He whispered, "My name the Mad Sixes, beast of no fixes,
running on wishes, call me clown vicious. Been a while
now, up the dial now, watch me, watch me, watch me
rile now. Owners and architects spinning their winnings,
building mad wormwood for the meek to trip in, and the
devils laugh, 'Drown, drown, drown.'"

He wrote on his arm:

MAYBE LIFE'S JUST GOT HERSELF TRICKED OUT IN THE ODD SHINY MOMENT
TO COVER THE TRUE BLUE UGLY,
THE ESSENCE OF THE 15.

chapter 16
TAMIKA

The Sykeses' apartment bathroom, Sunday, seventeen days before the hanging, 9:00 a.m. . . .

Mom bunched Mik's braids as Mik brushed her teeth. "Are you humming?" Mom said. "Careful, girlfriend. You keep up like this, folks might think you're happy."

Mik only went to church because if she didn't NaNa called demons out from the O House walls and prayed over her.

Dressed in their best jeans and coats, their Target shoes shined, mother, daughter and sometime Granny marched uphill toward a storefront church. Mik helped NaNa. The old woman hung full weight off Mik's arm. "Lawd, hill's steeper than the trail to Golgotha. Lawd, send an earthquake to level this devil hill."

When they came to Joe Knows's joint they found Jimmi

sitting on the sidewalk, head in hands. The bodega was closed, chain gate down, lights out, windows smashed. CRIME SCENE DO NOT CROSS tape X-ed the door.

NaNa touched Jimmi's shoulder. "James?"

Jimmi's face was swollen. He gently squeezed NaNa's hand, stepped onto his skateboard and gunned downhill without paying mind to the traffic.

"Joe get robbed?" Mom asked the owner of the ninety-nine cents store next door.

The man was opening his chain gate for a day that would be hectic with the after-church crowd. "Joe got dead."

"No," NaNa said.

"Fell asleep in his office with a lit cigarette in his mouth last night, the fire department figured. Burned the back of the building three stories up. Was a roomful of illegals on the third floor. Gate to the fire escape was rusted shut. Five Chinese living in a single room, you believe it? Hell we gonna do for takeout delivery now?" The old man spit. "Only good thing about it is we don't gotta deal with that stinking old German shepherd no more."

A flock of pigeons leaped from a power cable, tumbling into the sky and away.

Mik read Mom's lips: "Stop. Breathe."

Mik realized she was screaming.

The next morning Mom said, "You sure you don't want me to go with you?"

Mik signed, MA, I'LL GET THE INFORMATION, OKAY? TRUST ME.

"Huh?"

Fatima waited for her outside the school doors. They went to the doctor. He gave Mik a hearing test. "You're not a candidate for a cochlear implant. You don't have enough hearing loss to justify it. But you knew that already."

Mik nodded, signed, MY MOM WANTED ME TO ASK ABOUT THE PROCEDURE THEY'VE BEEN WORKING ON OVERSEAS THE LAST FEW YEARS.

"Artificial cochlear replacement. It's still highly experimental, but the results are promising. We could get you into the next trial. The surgery is subsidized by the manufacturer but not one hundred percent. It's expensive. In your case they would replace your left cochlea, the weaker one. They operate on only one side because—"

SOMETIMES THE SURGERY DOESN'T WORK, Mik signed.

The doctor nodded. "Let me see your hearing aids for a second? Yeah, these are terrible. I can prescribe you much better, much less obtrusive aids. Your hearing loss is severest in the high frequency range, but your low frequency reception is pretty good. Those aids you have now blocking your ear canals must drive you crazy when you speak. You hear a fuzzy echo when you talk, right?"

"She does not talk much," Fatima said.

"That's a shame," the doctor said. "I heard you out in the waiting room. You speak beautifully, Tamika. You would do really well with hearing aids where the sound receivers are in the ears. These are much smaller machines, quite comfortable, and you'll have far fewer ear infections.

The new aids would let you keep your ear canals open and maximize your natural hearing. You won't have those plugs stopping up your ears."

SO I WON'T BE ABLE TO BLOCK OUT THE SOUND ANYMORE? Mik signed.

The doctor squinted. "No."

"What did she say?" Fatima said.

"How much?" Mik said.

"Ten thousand. That's about twenty-five thousand less than the surgery."

That was twenty-five thousand Joe Knows dollars she could put toward an immigration lawyer. "Ten G's, huh? You know insurance doesn't cover hearing aids."

"Tell me about it. Look, you can go either way, surgery or new aids. It's up to you."

Fatima's landlord kept the basement heat at legal minimum, fifty-five degrees. The girls kept their coats on as they made dinner. "But why would you not want to hear?" Fatima said.

It would be too much, she wanted to say. *So many people making noise, so much garbage getting into my head. Folks like Shanelle, that idiot Jaekwon, dumping their nastiness on me. And the other folks, the ones crying out with complaints, trying to hitch up their problems to me, as if sharing their sadness will lighten their burdens instead of doubling them. As if I can do anything to cure their ills. Making me realize I'm powerless. I can barely get by with all that craziness blunted. Reality straight up? No thank you. Connecting to full-blown reality is tapping into full-blown insanity.*

She said none of these things. She said, "Spending that much money on aids is wrong. I'd rather put it to helping your sister come over here."

"That is not what this money is for," Fatima said. "You must honor Joe's wishes and put it toward your future. Besides, I am saving my money and my sister will be here soon enough." She read Mik's mind, part of it anyway. "No, still no word from her. But the mail is terrible over there with all of the displacement. Mik, the sign language teacher I told you about?"

"The one from the UN?"

"She said when Beethoven moved into deafness he held a tuning fork to his skull and compared it to what was vibrating up his fingers as he searched the piano keys." Fatima grabbed the clock radio from the shelf, put it into Mik's hands.

"This isn't Beethoven."

"No, but it is beautiful." Fatima cranked the volume.

Mik cradled the old radio. A hip-hop symphony throbbed in her arms, rib cage, spine, neck, popped and crackled in her old aids. The low frequency notes soothed her before the song started to fade. Mik cranked up the volume, but the music slipped further and further away. Her hearing aid batteries were dying.

chapter 17
JIMMI

The VA hospital, Tuesday, fifteen days
before the hanging, 5:00 p.m. . . .

A world without Joe Knows.

What kind of a world was that?

But if Joe were around, he would have said, *Kid, you can't give up. You gotta get back out there. Life's too short to waste time mourning. C'mon now, Jimmi, straighten up and fly right. Let's get to work.*

Jimmi tried. He showed up for his janitor gig, but he was such a mess his boss sent him home. "Jimmi, you're MIA how long, no call, no nothing, and now you come in looking like you slept in a Dumpster. Seriously, what's your problem, kid? You on drugs?"

"My problem is I'm *not* on drugs," Jimmi said.

The guy wanted to walk Jimmi to the emergency room,

but Jimmi took off. He wandered into the middle of the O Houses courtyard.

He stopped in a slant of sun, long and soft in the late afternoon. It felt like a kiss on his forehead.

"Jimmi. *Jimmi.*" Just aside the sunbeam, the angels called to him, Mik and Fatima.

Fatima yelled, "Wait there. We will come down to you."

He sat on a bench and watched folks rush around him to get home for dinner. Being in the middle of the sunny swirl felt great. The girls sat with him. "Then if you won't let us take you to the hospital," Mik said, "will you at least come up to the apartment for soup and a hot shower?"

"Your Moms won't like that."

"She at work."

"I don't think I ever heard you talk so much, Mik. You got a nice voice. What you two working on?"

"You mean art stuff?" Mik said.

"As a team?" Fatima said.

"Nothing just yet," Mik said.

"Nothing, huh?" Jimmi smiled. He hopped onto his board and skated away backward, bowing to them as he rounded the corner. Out of the sunlight he felt sick.

chapter 18
TAMIKA

A classroom, Wednesday, fourteen days
before the hanging, 11:00 a.m. . . .

"Yo woman, not for nothin', but the way you *talk*, dag.
Deaf is sexy." Jaekwon cornered Mik as art ended, after
everybody else had run out.

"Get over yourself." Mik tried not too hard to sneak out
of his pin job. "Lemme go before I scream."

He licked his lips and lowered his face to hers, cinnamon
on his breath. Mik rarely chewed gum because it played
hell with her ears when her aids were in, but when she
did chew, cinnamon was her favorite.

He was too much, that extra hunk of cake they tempt
you with after your stomach aches full. You know it'll make you
sick once it's in you, but how good it tastes in your mouth,
going down. She hated herself for a shallow shell of a woman
as she closed her eyes, waited, lips soft, ready.

The kiss never came.

When she opened her eyes he was out the door. Shanelle, back from suspension, stood in his place. She had her phone in Mik's face, a snapshot of Mik, eyes shut, puckered up for a big air kiss. "I'm-a e-mail this to like a thousand people."

Mik took in the crowd of howling kids, grateful she remembered to turn off her hearing aids at the beginning of class. She pushed through the mob.

Jaekwon chased after her, got in her face for her to read the lips she'd tried to kiss. "Yo Mik. I just kiddin', yo. Shanelle dare me to do it. Here." He slapped ten dollars into her hand. "That's my winnings. I want you to have it, dig? C'mon, take me to Taco B."

She shoved him. "Punk."

"Why you gotta play it so mad serious all the time, yo? It was a *joke*, girl. You can't laugh at yourself a little, yo?"

She pushed on, flipping up her palm, talk to the hand style.

"A'ight, be like that then." Jaekwon shrugged, headed back to Shanelle. He was cold to her until she grabbed his jaw and tongued him deep.

Mik slipped out the cafeteria door to hit the park for some clear air, maybe to cut the rest of her classes too.

The G chased her, tripping over his low-slung jeans. They fell to his knees. His boxer shorts were two sizes too big. He yanked up his pants and pulled near-dead flowers from his backpack.

"For?" Mik said. She clicked on her aids.

"Saving my lame butt from Shanelle the other day. I been

holding 'em since, afraid to give 'em to you. Spilt the water cup in my locker. My math's dumb plus wet now. Spent, like, four dollars on those. Deli's getting mad expensive."

She grabbed his hand, pulled him behind the Dumpster, kissed him. She pulled back to look at him.

"Like, why you crying?" he said.

She kissed him again. He kissed back, his teeth chattering. She caught her lip on his braces. He fumbled hard at her breasts. His want for her enchanted her. She felt slippery and fevery and as if she were falling backward, and she jumped up and went.

"Wait," he said.

"I'm sorry, G," she said.

"I love you," he said. "Serious, Mik. I'm-a die I don't marry you."

"What's G stand for?"

"Gale." The kid was breathless. "Like the wind. I can't believe I got to kiss Mik Sykes."

"Gale," she said to herself. His name made her love him all the more, but friends style. You can't be *in* love with somebody when you feel sorry for him. "You're too good for me."

"Yo, I can be *bad*, woman. It's because y'all are like two inches taller than me, right? I'm on'y four*teen*, yo. I'm-a be growing soon, girl. I'm-a grow a *foot* for you."

"I'm so sorry."

"That was the best thirty seconds of my loser life. I *love* you, baby."

She backed away, feeling worse about this kiss than the one that hadn't happened.

chapter 19
FATIMA

Bronx-Orange high school, front
courtyard, Wednesday, fourteen days
before the hanging, 3:00 p.m. . . .

Fatima leaned against the mailbox to write her sister a letter.

Two weeks now and no word from the east.

She dropped the letter into the box as Mik hurried from school.

"Good day?"

"Perfect," Mik said.

"You are a fantastically bad liar. Show me your sketch."

Mik pulled a roll of drawing paper from a cardboard tube.

Fatima studied the drawing topped with a teacher's writing: *Fabulous work, Mik.* "More empty streets." Fatima dragged Mik uphill by the hand.

"Where we going?"

"I think you will be a remarkable artist someday very soon, but only if you learn to do one thing first. You must let *people* into your dreamworld. Come, I will show you something. Something you don't know about you."

chapter 20
TAMIKA

The VA hospital, Wednesday, fourteen
days before the hanging, 3:15 p.m. . . .

Fatima introduced Mik to the dude who ran the volunteer
programs. He was all military with his creased khakis and
dry-cleaned button-down. "Friend of Fatima's, friend of
mine." Firm handshake, hard, cold face. "I got no problem
with you hanging with Fatima in the classroom."

Mik hadn't thought there would have been. Dude was
creepy.

In the classroom: a bunch of kids around a table, adults
in the background.

"Hello, my little ones." Fatima tickled the kids. "This
is my friend Mik. She is very cool. Make my friend feel
welcome, please. Say hello."

They did. The littlest boy said, "What's those things on
your ears?"

"She is hard of hearing," Fatima said.

The boy said, "My Pops got hurt in the desert. He's upstairs. He's sleeping. Someday he's gonna wake up, though."

Mik sat next to the kid.

"Can we make giraffes, Fatima?" a girl said.

"Can we? We must." Fatima handed out sheets of newspaper. The kids copied her as they folded, ripped and crimped the newspaper into a herd of giraffes.

The little boy, the one whose father was upstairs, was lost. His giraffe had two legs and two necks.

Mik showed him where he went wrong.

Fatima watched her help the kid. "Mik, will you lead the class for us?"

Mik looked around the room, twenty kids, another twenty adults, eighty eyes on her. She signed to Fatima, I CAN'T DO IT.

"You can and you will," Fatima said.

Mik signed, NO WAY.

"Where is my little Juliet? Yes, there you are. Will you show us how to make lions?"

They walked along the park. "The children loved you, Sister Mik. Did you know you were such a wonderful teacher?"

"One-on-one, I don't mind so much, but with a crowd—"

"Next time you will teach all the students."

"Anybody ever tell you you're kind of bossy?"

"I have to be."

The following Sunday morning Mik woke with an aching face. She smiled even as she remembered the cause of her pain—all that smiling this past week, helping Fatima at the hospital. She stretched in the sunlight warming her bedcovers.

The happy feeling didn't last.

Mom came in. "Y'all shower and dress for church."

"Can't wait."

"You can pray for Joe Knows, Mika."

"That'll bring him back."

"Who birthed you? Are you my child?"

chapter 21
FATIMA

Church, Sunday, ten days before the
hanging, noon...

Fatima woke two hours early to be sure she would sell out
her papers in time to go to church with Mik, Mom, and
NaNa.

Mik whispered, "Why would you come here willingly?"

"For fun."

"For what?" Mik said.

"Girls, hush," Mom said.

The music was wonderful. Everyone clapped and sang
along. NaNa swayed and sang louder than anyone else.
Fatima watched as Mik adjusted her hearing aids to hear
the guitar player, her eyes on the guitarist's fingers pluck-
ing magic from the strings. Mik grimaced.

Fatima nudged Mik and pointed to the skylight.

Mik keyed her phone: ?

Fatima signed, PRETTY DAY. She thought, *I hope the weather will be this nice when we visit Liberty.*

It wasn't. Fatima gave away the papers she couldn't sell this cold rainy Monday holiday honoring the American veterans. She was at Mik's by noon. They helped NaNa pack the sandwiches she made for their trip.

Mom walked in tired from work. "Hey."

"Mom." Fatima hugged Sandrine Sykes. The woman's arms were strong, like Fatima's mother's.

"Drine Sykes, you ever been to the Statue of Liberty?" NaNa said. "Me neither."

"Y'all be back for dinner," Mom said. "Teesha called in sick, I'm to cover her overnight, but NaNa got the chicken out for a good one here, okay? Hey girls, y'all don't go wandering now. Mika, you hear me? If you won't get the new aids, then at least keep the old ones on. Don't you *Tt* me, missy. Look at her, rolling her eyes. Y'all watch out for them tourists. They come over here acting all ignorant, trick you into showing 'em around, next thing you know they buying you dinner and drinks with drugs slipped in them, and you're back at their hotel, *no* idea how you got there or why half y'all's clothes are on the floor."

NaNa threw her arms around the girls. "They be fine. Nobody-a mess with this Fatima woman. Y'all cut quite a figure. You too, Mika. Just look *mean*. Yes, like that. My girls are *fierce*."

They trained down to the ferry, sipping cheap beer from a brown bag.

Mik said and signed, "I feel bad, corrupting you."

"Do you think I am such a nerd?" Fatima signed the words letter by letter with her hand. "Correct?"

"Yes to both."

A homeless man begged. They gave him NaNa's sandwiches.

"You think he's okay?" Mik said.

She knew Mik was speaking of Jimmi. "Yes. You?"

"Yes. You're lying to me, aren't you?"

"Yes. You too?"

"Yes."

They sipped the beer, but without laughter now.

The ferry was nearly empty, the fog thick, the water rough. They ate concession-stand pizza. It was hot and delicious. They bought tourist T-shirts and silly foam hats, Liberty's spiked crown. They took pictures of each other posing like Liberty with Mik's phone. A tourist took a shot of them together, twin Liberties. A little drunk, they talked nonstop about happy things, the kids at the VA hospital, handsome boys—

"That one is staring at you," Mik said.

Fatima turned. "I think he is staring at *you*."

"Am I red? Stop looking at them."

Fatima waved. "Hello."

Mik slapped down Fatima's hand. "Look, here they come now."

The boy and his friend sat next to the girls. "What up?" the first boy said. He nudged Mik.

Mik blushed. Fatima laughed.

"We wondering what y'all hiding under that scarf," the other said.

"Wouldn't you like to know?" Fatima winked.

"Fa*ti*ma," Mik said.

"Where y'all headed?" the boy said. He tried to hold Fatima's hand.

"I believe you must know this boat only goes to the Statue of Liberty." Fatima playfully slapped away the boy's hand.

Mik dragged Fatima into the bathroom. "Put a leash on you, girl."

"Do we have any more beer?" Fatima said.

"*No.*" Mik undid her hair in the dented metal mirror and tied it back to pin her ears.

Fatima washed her hands as she watched Mik. "I do not know why you hide them. Look at these ears, fantastic. They are so big. I would love to decorate them with shiny things."

"That's only gonna make folks look at 'em more."

"Exactly."

An announcement came over the PA system: *Due to the inclement weather, we will be forced to turn the boat around. This is as close as we get to Liberty today, folks. Take pictures while you can.*

"What did he say?" Mik said.

The ferry turning broadside, Fatima and Mik ran to the boat railing to glimpse the Great Lady. She was far away. Fog covered all but her feet.

Mik hung her arm on Fatima's shoulder.

"You have to laugh," Fatima said. And she did.

chapter 22
TAMIKA

The Bronx West strip, Monday, nine
days before the hanging, 7:00 p.m. . . .

Laughing arm in arm they skipped the strip across from the
O Houses. The strip's lights airbrushed the night red and
green. A boy whistled at Fatima. "Two boys flirted with
me today—a record. Why are they looking at me?"

Mik pointed to Fatima's reflection in a parked car's glass.
Fatima's reflection smiled back at them. "Your eyes," Mik
said. "They're crinkling."

"Yours too."

Mik nodded.

A pack of girls shoved Fatima before they ran off. Their
screams blew out Mik's hearing aids. They said something
about horror, or terror.

"Did they just call you a—"

"Terrorist."

"Yo!" Mik said. "Come back here and say that."

"Do not bait them," Fatima said.

"Folks are ignorant. You gotta lose the scarf."

"Impossible. It was my mother's." Fatima pulled the shawl higher to cover her scar.

"They're coming back," Mik said.

"Please do not even think about calling the police."

"Then let's duck into a store." They went into Jimmy Jazz's, a HELP WANTED sign by the register. Mik asked for an application.

The manager stole a peek at Mik's hearing aids as he handed her the paper.

"I gotta take it home to get my Moms to sign it, right?" Mik said.

"Either way," the dude said.

Mik nodded. Yeah, she wasn't getting this job.

The dude eyed Fatima. "You probably want one too, huh?"

Fatima looked around the store, smiled, shook no.

They went out, the posse gone.

"They play fun music in there," Fatima said. "Maybe someday if I win a green card—"

A dude cut in front of them with a German shepherd that looked like Joe's Tranquilito. Mik went to pet it. The dog snapped at her. The dog's owner pulled a badge on a necklace from his shirt. "We're working here."

Mik nodded, backed up. Fatima was gone. Mik hunted the strip. Fatima had backpedaled into the shadows under the elevated train. "I must go," she said.

"What about dinner? NaNa's expecting you."

"They are across the street too, the police, in front of your building."

"Girl, they're not looking for you. Those are drug-sniffing dogs. Those guys are narcs. You got to stop being so paranoid."

Red and blue lights peppered the building behind Fatima. A siren chirped. An NYPD cruiser slow-rolled the strip. The cop in the shotgun seat spotted folks with a hand-held searchlight.

"Sister Mik, I have to bounce."

"Wait for me then."

"No, go home. NaNa—"

Mik stuck her phone in Fatima's hand. "Call her, tell her I'm sleeping over. Except we won't be sleeping."

"Please explain."

"We better stop for coffee first. C'mon. We'll get you to Liberty yet."

They hooked into the alley, then uphill into the dark park.

Mik and Fatima studied the Liberty brochure in the flashlight. The statue's official name was *Liberty Enlightening the World.*

From Fatima's cart they unloaded the buckets of old paint they had taken from the ghost house a week and a half earlier to paint Fatima's yard. They lined them up in front of the abandoned NYPD garage door. "The cops never come here anymore," Mik said. "I promise."

"I trust you," Fatima said. "I do."

They set up the accordion ladder they found with the paint.

The streetlights were dead. They took turns lighting the garage for each other with the flashlight. In the dim light and over the gang graffiti they painted the statue, adding six ultraviolet wings to Liberty as she looked over an expressionist cityscape. Then in every color they painted part of what Fatima said she wished she had seen more than anything else: the plaque inside Liberty's pedestal, Emma Lazarus's poem. Fatima had memorized it long before she came to America.

Here at our sea-washed, sunset gates shall stand
A mighty woman with a torch, whose flame
Is the imprisoned lightning, and her name
Mother of Exiles

They did not paint over one part of the wall, where years earlier Jimmi's patchwork of hearts and clocks had come together to spell out LOVE KILLS TIME.

Fatima put up her fist for a knuckle bump.

Mik bumped her. "Like that."

Every Third had followed them here. The cat rubbed against Mik's legs, hissing at her. They had picked up McDonald's on the way but forgot to eat as the painting drew them in. The cat didn't mind that the chicken sandwiches were five hours cold. He scratched at the bag. The girls pulled the meat from the fried breading and set it before Every Third. They stepped back to watch the rickety little cat eat at the feet of the great winged lady.

chapter 23
JIMMI

The cave, Tuesday, eight days before
the hanging, 3:00 a.m. . . .

Jimmi didn't believe in the next world. Why then did
he have the feeling Joe was looking over his shoulder as he
chiseled the cave floor with a bent screwdriver and a
brick?

ONE.
LAST.
TIME.

He rested his forehead on the floor, whispered into the
dust, "Tomorrow I'm back on the wagon, Joe. I swear."

He went to buy until he remembered he was broke. He
waited in the alley.

The low-level methamphetamine dealer rushed out of his tenement. He hopped into the Navigator he'd parked in front of a dead hydrant two minutes earlier.

The car gunning out of sight, Jimmi slipped into the building, up to the second floor, the last crib on the left. He stuck an awl into the lock. One shot with the side of a cloth-covered hammer, *thunk*, twist, and he was in with a lot less noise than you'd think.

He left the lights off and made his way by feel into the kitchen, to the cabinet where the dealer kept his stash.

The cabinet had no stash tonight. He was about to jet when something in the back of the cabinet caught his eye—a dim glint. The microwave clock light reflected off something peeking out from behind a fat bag of sugar. Jimmi shoved the sugar aside and found a Colt .45, old-school silver.

Interesting.

You come looking for drugs and you find a pistola.

He hadn't held one since his time in the desert. He hadn't wanted to use it, but he did. He told Joe about that night, the botched raid. Joe understood. Joe'd had to bust a few caps in his day. Joe *did* know. Not anymore though.

Now there was nobody to talk to.

Maybe this was God's way of telling Jimmi the time had come to end this life filled with too many lousy surprises.

He checked the safety, then the wheel, chock-full o' bullies. He tipped the cylinder, letting the slugs backslide out of their chambers. The .45 caliber bullet was a showstopper all right. He pocketed the slugs and tucked the gun into his waistband.

Creaking behind him, the bedroom door opened. The lights popped on. The dealer's big dude brother, tall as Jimmi and twice as thick, said, "Kill you, junkie."

Jimmi swung past the dude for the back bedroom, kicked the door shut behind him, jumped the sill as the door blew in. Clear of the window he rolled hard onto the fire escape. He dropped down to the back courtyard and sprinted into the alley. The dealer's brother chased, a nine in hand.

Out on the street, kids were playing punchball in the dawn light. A five-year-old—maybe—ran hard into the street to catch a fly.

Jimmi doubled back and pushed the little kid clear of a cab skidding sideways. The cab clipped Jimmi. He rolled up the hood, over the shield, dropped off the back. He would ache everywhere tomorrow. He looked at the kid. "Tell me you all right."

The kid's shock gave way to tears of embarrassment. He was clean.

Jimmi scrambled for the dropped gun. He ducked into the highway traffic to lose the dealer's brother. Out of breath the dude stopped chasing. He yelled, "Crazy Jimmi, you a dead man."

The morning sun took a bite out of the tenement cliff. Jimmi disappeared in the glare. He limped into the under-pass and dropped into the gutter alongside the Amtrak rails. He whistled "Amazing Grace" as he studied the Colt. He cocked the hammer, *ka-click*. "How sweet the sound that saved a wretch like me."

chapter 24
TAMIKA

School, Mik's lunch spot under the stairs, Tuesday, eight days before the hanging . . .

She stared at the bank check Mom put in her hand that morning. The audiologist had called. The new hearing aids were ready for pickup. She calculated how much of Joe Knows's money would be left after she paid the doctor and wondered if that plus her savings from her homework business would be enough for the immigration lawyer. No. She'd need help from Mom and then some.

A velvet box floated into her lap. She followed the string up to Gale. He winked to her from the stairwell landing. She had been hiding from him, but now she tapped a spot of bench next to her. He sat.

Mik eyed the book-size box. "Big engagement ring," she said.

"Better than that," he said.

She opened the box: a pen. It was not the one she wanted. It was nicer. She fought a want to cut her lip on his braces again. "I can't accept this."

"Why?"

"Homeboy, you can't buy your way into making somebody love you."

"Why not?"

"Gale, I can't commit to a, you know, whachamacallit."

"Relationship?"

"Can y'all settle for us being friends?"

"I still love you, though.

"Lemme see your homework."

"Please keep the pen?"

She mussed his fledgling braids. "You got a lot of free math coming your way."

Life was getting complicated. Now she had *three* friends to worry about. She gave him half her PBJ. They ate in silence.

Fatima waited right out front. So did a girl from Shanelle's posse. The chick waved to Mik, the wave turning into a salute, middle finger only.

"The universal sign," Fatima said.

"You don't want to try them on here?" the doctor said. Mik shook no.

"But we should calibrate them."

I'LL FIGURE IT OUT. I WANT TO BE HOME THE FIRST TIME, Mik signed.

The doctor frowned, looked to Fatima.

Fatima shrugged.

THANK YOU, Mik signed. She put the new aids in her pocket and left.

Back in the O Houses, they hung in Mik's room. She slid the new aids out of their case. A quarter of the size of her old bud-style aids, they were two thin tubes that left her ear canals wide open.

"You should wait for Mom, no?" Fatima said.

Mik clicked on the aids. If sound were color, everything was too bright. If it were a hand, it scratched the backs of Mik's eyes with sharpened nails. The metallic sizzle in her throat reminded her of the time that girl in second grade tricked her into licking the top of a nine-volt battery.

Someone was clinking dishes as she washed them in the apartment across the breezeway. Mik felt as if the woman were smashing the plates over Mik's head.

A baby screeched from another apartment. He might as well have been screaming in Mik's ear.

Every sound in the world demanded Mik's full attention. Hundreds, thousands of fingers poked her, *Hey, Yo, Check me out, Yo I said, Listen to* me, *Hey—*

Everything was "too real."

She clicked off the aids. Her ear canals open, the sound didn't cut out.

No more silky silence.

Everything far away but not far away enough. Unclear. She felt naked. She cupped her ears.

Fatima nudged her. "No?"

Mik put her old aids back in. "Why'd she make me do this? Wasting all that money."

"Maybe you will try again later."

"Maybe not."

Fatima nodded. "Regardless of whether you wear the new aids or don't?"

"Yeah?"

"Love Mom."

DOC LIED, Mik signed. THEY'RE UNCOMFORTABLE.

"What?" Mom said.

Mik hung the dishtowel and went into her room. She pulled out her sketchbook and the new pen. She didn't care that Mom followed and watched her from the door.

"Mika, you just have to get used to them. Can you at least take the old ones out of your ears?"

"*Mom*, just . . . Can you leave me alone? Please, okay?"

Mom nodded. "I just want you to know, you hurt me, girlfriend."

"It has to be my decision—"

"Not that. Y'all do what you want with the aids. But the fact that you didn't wait for me to be here with you when you turned them on? After all that time, the two of us working to get you to this point? All those hours I'm double-shifting, Mika? The *years*? How could you do that to me?" Mom left.

Mik followed her to her bedroom, knocked. She tried the door, locked.

chapter 25
JIMMI

Jimmi's cave, Tuesday, eight days before
the hanging, 11:00 p.m. . . .

He was having a full-blown conversation with himself. "You won't. I *will*. You ain't got the heart. I won't in a second."

He put the gun to his heart, pulled the trigger, *click*.

He'd been doing this on and off for the last day, rehearsal for the real deal.

He'd seen friends and enemies do it overseas. The rope and knife left grimaces on the corpses. The gun left no sign of regret. He slipped a bullet into the chamber and put the gun to his temple. He asked God to send him a sign about whether or not to snap the trigger. None came.

He cocked the hammer, clamped his eyes, said, "If a better world than this." He tried to see that world. He couldn't. Instead he sensed what a blindworm must feel when it digs too deep: gritty dark.

In that dark came a flash of Joe Knows, a scrap of memory: Joe laughing the time Jimmi brought him a cake for his birthday.

Jimmi put the gun down. He had to do one last thing for Joe.

chapter 26
FATIMA

McDonald's, Wednesday, seven days
before the hanging, 4:00 p.m. . . .

While Mik was in the bathroom Fatima studied a free
Spanish paper. Articles were translated into English on
the opposite page. Fatima taught herself the language as
she hunted for news from the east. Word of Africa's troubles had dropped from print for the most part, at least
from the rag Fatima sold, but sometimes *El Día* covered
world events.

Not today.

Mik came back. Fatima showed her how to make a dog
out of a burger wrapper. This would be today's lesson at the
VA. YOU WILL LEAD THE CLASS? Fatima signed.

NEXT TIME.

"You have been saying 'next time' many times now. But
no pressure."

"No, never." Mik squinted. "That dude at the hospital, the head volunteer guy, he kind of creeps me out."

"Why?"

"You don't worry he'll rat you out?"

"Never. He is, how you say, off the hook cool."

"'Off the hook,' huh?"

"I am becoming very down with it. Now you must punch my knuckles."

Mik bumped her.

Two cops came in. One checked out Fatima's headscarf. He looked away to the dollar menu, no big deal. Still, Fatima said, "We should get to the hospital."

Outside, Mik said, "Let's check with Jimmi's boss to see if he came back to work."

"I worry that he . . . " Fatima's eyes stopped on something across the street.

They crossed the strip to read a poster taped to the whitewashed glass of a vacant storefront: *DID YOU KNOW THAT YOU COULD MAKE 5-10K/MONTH WORKING AS AN INFORMATION SPECIALIST FOR THE U.S. DEPT OF IMMIGRATION?*

"Informants," Fatima said. "They are recruiting informants."

Mik ripped the poster down.

chapter 27
TAMIKA

Mik's bedroom, Wednesday, seven days
before the hanging, 7:00 p.m. . . .

She studied the paper dolls she made that afternoon with
Fatima and the kids at the VA: elephants and baboons,
animals Mik had seen only behind zoo barricades but
Fatima had seen in her country's streets. She laid out the
figures on top of her newest sketch, the Orange Houses as
seen from the roof of the abandoned doctor's house behind
Fatima's.

Mik shut her eyes, whispered, "If a city without
walls . . ."

She saw herself in her dream world. As she walked the
streets they turned from ink to pavement, the penned
buildings to brick and glass. She touched the newsprint
animals and they came to life. A zebra herd grazed the park
lawn. Monkeys hung out in the playground. Pelicans and

pigeons flocked as one over the Orange Houses. A gust spun the birds—

Mom created a draft when she opened the bedroom door. She was dressed for work. "I left the Lean Cuisines in the microwave on thaw."

"NaNa down yet?"

Mom shook no.

"I'll bring her dinner up."

Mom eyed the new hearing aids on Mik's desk as she closed the door.

NaNa nursed her cold in bed. Mik brought her soup. NaNa took off her glasses and rubbed her eyes. "Swear I'm going blind. Child, I'm in a jam for my Bible study tomorrow. Read this for me. Micah 7, let's do 18 and 19."

Mik read, "'God, who are you, that you pardon and forgive us? You show us mercy. You show us compassion. You throw away our sins and banish our crimes to the bottom of the sea.'"

"I must tell you, it's so nice to hear you speaking again. When you were young we could not get you to hush up. Been awful quiet these last ten years." NaNa flipped the book to another dog-eared page. "And this, the underlined."

"Psalms, 104, verses 15 and 16. 'Man's days are like grass. He blossoms like wildflowers. Then the wind blows over the field and the flowers dry up and fade and are forgotten.'"

"What all you think that means?"

"Bible study, huh?"

NaNa blew the heat off her soup. "Sort it out for me."

Mik rolled her eyes. "I'd say the psalm means time is short, do what you got to do."

"What about the Micah?"

"*I* don't know, NaNa. I got homework—"

"More than God, you know whom you got to ask for forgiveness? Whom you got to go to for compassion, to show mercy? To give all y'all's love?"

"Who?"

"You." NaNa nailed Mik with bright eyes.

"Me?"

The next day Jaekwon waited out in the hall for Mik. "I got news you need to know."

"Step off."

"Why you gotta be such a hater, yo? Ever hear of forgive and forget? You fix your hair different or something?"

She ran her hand over her do: same old crow's nest. She hooked into the stairwell.

"I came to warn you, Shanelle getting ready to posse up on you."

"What I ever did to her?"

"Getting her suspended ain't enough? Her aunt belt-whipped her. She got drunk and crying last night, say you make her feel stupit."

"*I* do?"

"She knows you're going places she ain't. She say she catch you without that bodyguard chick, she-a dead you." Jae shrugged. "Sha got mad head problems, man, you don't know. Chick is *wack*."

96

"Then why y'all hang with her?"

"I really gotta tell you? Yo baby, that's what being a boy is all about."

Gale rolled up, wimpy chest puffed out. "I *know* you ain't stepping to my Mik, son. You step to my girl, you step to *me*."

Giant Jae put up his hands in mock surrender. "Okay Killuh, I don't want no trouble."

Mik hooked Gale's arm. "Walk me to class."

Mik's arm through his, Gale strutted. "Stomp that Romeo's punk butt."

"Easy, hero."

As Mik stepped through the school doors into the front courtyard a rock zipped past Fatima's head.

Crew Shanelle rolled up the sidewalk. "Deaf bitch can't get no real friends, she stuck with a Zulu terrorist." Shanelle got in Fatima's face. "You ain't *nothin'*."

Fatima reached into her shawl.

Shanelle reached for her back pocket, a bulge that said box cutter.

Fatima drew her hand from her scarf. A flock of Day-Glo butterflies spun in the breeze. In the afternoon light their sequined wings dazzled Sha's posse. The girls fell on the butterflies as if they were spilled piñata candy.

"It's newspaper," one girl said. "Painted newspaper." She drew her phone, keyed it for a new entry. "Yo," she said to Fatima, "I got a birthday party coming for my niece. We was gonna get a clown, but y'all gonna work it instead. My sistuh got cash money, yo. What's y'all's numbuh?"

"Zero," Fatima said.

"How's that?"

"I do not have a phone."

"How y'all talk to your friends?"

"With my mouth."

The girl nodded. "Cool."

"Don't be talking to her," Sha said.

"Sha*nelle*, *chill* yo. Why you gotta order everybody around all the time yo? I'm-a get suspended for *you*? You got a problem with her, then *you* step to her."

"Step to you too—"

"What*ev*uh. You ain't all that. C'mon, y'all."

All but two of the girls ditched Sha. The new leader wrote her number on a gum wrapper and slapped it into Fatima's hand. "Call me, I put you to work."

"Y'all are trippin'," Sha called after her former crew. "Y'all are *loose*." She backed off, miming a gun at Mik as she went.

Mik tried to stop trembling, then realized she wasn't. Her arm hooked through Mik's, Fatima was shaking.

"Today Mik will lead us," Fatima said.

Fifty or so kids, adults, vets packed the room. One dude was catatonic in a wheeler, twisted in a mess of tubes and bags.

"Teacher, teach," Fatima said.

Mik clicked on her old aids. "Today we're gonna make butterflies."

"Nah, butterflies are for chicks," a boy said.

"Butterflies are too easy," said a girl.

"Let's make angels," another girl said.

"All y'all ever want to do is make angels," Mik said. "How about we make each other?"

"Too hard," a boy said.

"We're angels without the wings. Pick a partner."

Mik helped the kids create their parents. Fatima showed the parents how to put together their kids. Mik helped everyone draw faces onto the dolls. Drawing eyes came easily to her today.

A girl tugged on Mik's sleeve. "You have nice teeth."

Within an hour, the dolls strolled a city street Mik and Fatima built from wrapping paper, rolled cardboard and tissue boxes.

The dude who ran the volunteer program watched from the corner, arms folded, his face grim.

chapter 28
JIMMI

Joe Knows's fire-gutted bodega,
Thursday, six days before the hanging,
11:00 p.m. . . .

He broke in by way of the back alley. His hands shook. He couldn't remember the last time he'd eaten. What was left in the bodega was melted and smoked. Joe's body was gone but his old wooden chair was still here, an ash heap now. The charred skeleton of Joe's dog Tranquilito lay where Joe's feet would have been as he slumped dead in the chair. The skeleton looked as if it had been dipped into chunky tar.

Some of Joe lay in these ashes.

Jimmi scooped cinder and silt into a coffee can. He was dizzy when he stood too quickly from his crouch. He put the can in his backpack and staggered toward the side door. When he stepped into the alley, a flashlight drilled him. His hands were black with ash as he wiped his eyes.

The cops cuffed him, read him his rights. They were tired but nice, nicer when they went through his wallet and found his VA card.

"What say we let him go?" the one cop said to the other.

The other cop looked up at the apartment lights across the back alley, the people leaning out the windows. "Too late now."

"You guys got any candy on you?" Jimmi said. "Gum? Gonna pass out if I don't get something sweet into me."

"I'll write this up as trespassing," the first cop said. "You won't lose your VA benefits."

"Doesn't matter anyway," Jimmi said.

"You're not gonna eat that?"

"You are?" The prisoner nudged his gluey detention center breakfast toward Jimmi, hungry for seconds.

Everyone else looked wrecked after the long night behind bars, but Jimmi felt great. Fed, rested, warm, his mind had cleared. The cops had arranged a shower for him. He felt new, shiny.

A guard nodded to him. "Let's go."

At the desk they gave him what he brought in: his backpack and Joe's ashes. As he stepped out into the sunlight he felt as if Life loved him a little, but the feeling didn't last.

chapter 29
FATIMA

A diner across from the courthouse,
Friday, five days before the hanging,
5:00 p.m. . . .

Mik and Fatima watched for Jimmi from the diner window. Fatima would get no closer to the police coming in and out of the courthouse. Jimmi helped NaNa down the stone steps, across the street, into the diner booth. He had listed her as his family contact. He was gaunt under the army uniform NaNa brought from the halfway house.

"Judge give him an earful," NaNa said. "Woman made me swear we'd get him back to the hospital. You'd never let me break my word with God, James?"

Jimmi winked.

"Incorrigible," NaNa said. "Order big now and eat up. Put the meat back on you."

Jimmi's smile was a lie. His eyes were tired as he looked first at Fatima, then Mik. "What y'all working on?"

"Mik is teaching the children with me," Fatima said. "She is a wonderful teacher."

Jimmi's smile was genuine for a moment before it died. "Word from your sister?"

Fatima shook no.

He nodded, his eyes on a sunburst caught in a parked car's windshield.

"Let us take you to the hospital, Jimmi," Mik said.

"So they can drug me back into the great big lie?"

"What lie?" Mik said.

"That everything's okay." He kissed NaNa's cheek as he left.

"Shouldn't we stop him?" Mik said.

"Only he can stop him," NaNa said.

The women watched as Jimmi paused in the middle of the concourse sidewalk. He reached into the glare reflecting off the car and pulled a flyer from a windshield wiper. He folded it into an angel, set it in the diner window's outer sill so it looked in at Fatima. He hurried away.

Fatima went out for the angel, but the wind had taken it.

Mik followed her, signed, YOU ALL RIGHT?

Fatima signed, I WILL HAVE TO BE.

103

chapter 30
TAMIKA

The Sykeses' apartment, Sunday, three
days before the hanging, 3:45 a.m. ...

Mik headed out.

"Showered and dressed at this hour?" Mom said as she
dressed for work, her eyes on the TV.

"Helping Fatima with her papers."

Closed captions flashed over the TV screen as a sena-
tor said: WE OVERRODE THE FIRST VETO, AND
WE'LL OVERRIDE THIS ONE TOO. THE PASSAGE
OF THE BILL WILL BE A VICTORY FOR THE
AMERICAN WORKER, NOT TO MENTION OUR
NATIONAL SECURITY. The news anchor said the new
law would force local cops to report illegals to Immigra-
tion.

This young, the day had a strange feel. The dealers and gangbangers were done for the night. The early shift zombies yawned as they marched for the train. The overnighters yawned as they limped off it. The rummies were off to the side, sleeping on the heat grates. The light from the streetlamps was intense. With fewer folks' shadows on them, the sidewalks were both brighter and lonelier. Mik's want for more people on the street surprised her.

She turned the alley corner into Fatima's yard. Fatima was at the doorjamb trying to coax the old cat inside with cheese.

"Sister Mik, you bring me the sunrise."

Mik wondered if she should tell Fatima about the new immigration bill. What good would knowing about it do? She petted the cat. "Still won't come in, huh?"

"Soon, when the weather turns colder."

They lugged the leftover Sunday editions uphill to the hospital for next week's doll-making classes. Few words passed between them, but Mik felt no pressure to fill the quiet. They went to church to help with NaNa's soup kitchen.

A young homeless man said, "Miracle. Hot food. Thank you, darlin'." He let Mik put just one pancake onto his paper plate. Hunched and head down, he shuffled out the door and into the sun whiting out the sidewalk.

"What's wrong?" Mom said. She was still in her Dunkin' uniform.

"Worried about Jimmi," Mik said.

Mom frowned.

The reverend tapped the microphone. "Let's do the scripture. Who's got a song?"

Folks grabbed their books and sang.

"Fatima has a lovely singing voice," Mom said, her eyes darting from Mik's left ear to her right, the old aids still plugging them up.

chapter 31
JIMMI

The park gates, Monday, two days
before the hanging, 5:00 a.m. . . . .

He hunted the sky for a patch not milked with streetlamp and found a fading scrap of dark. He wondered if the dim pinpoint in it was a star or a plane. "Or an asteroid come to blow away our troubles."

He stepped into the park a wanderer. Since Saturday he was looking for a place to lay Joe Knows's ashes. Determined to find the most peaceful spot, he would know it when he saw it. He would travel the park's eleven hundred acres if he had to. He knew many of them. He'd been coming here since he was a kid, whenever he felt lost.

He watched a girl scream laughter as her mother pushed her swing.

Jimmi tried not to think how he would feel when night came and everybody disappeared. He scanned the sky. The sun was in the west. He couldn't recall the hours that had passed as he tramped the trails from one wildwood grove to the next.

So many folks were in the park this warm fall afternoon—kids running, mothers chasing. Where were all the fathers?

He headed for the cliffs, remembering from years ago a slant of sunset that lit the fields up there reddish gold.

Nobody ever came up this way. The climb was steep and the path unmarked as it curved with the ledge. Joe would find peace here.

No.

The field wasn't as he'd remembered. Here were boosted cars now. Stripped and torched they would ugly the meadow for ages. Methamphetamine vials crackled under his soles like bubble pack.

He figured he should just step off the cliff. He took a last look at the world, his eyes stopping on that abandoned NYPD garage just east of the O Houses. The angels had blessed it with a six-winged Statue of Liberty.

The girls were doing it, creating the only thing that mattered—not the mural, though that was stunning with its flying Liberty. The only thing that mattered was what had made them paint it.

Maybe this bit of wonder would be enough to carry him

through the night into another day of wandering with Joe's ashes.

Maybe.

He watched a hawk bullet the dying sun and thought of the Colt .45 waiting for him in his cave. He'd fire it right after he buried Joe. He'd do it tomorrow night.

chapter 32
FATIMA

An immigration lawyer's office, Tuesday,
the day before the hanging, 4:00
p.m. . . .

"Your only shot is an emergency asylum petition," the lawyer said. "No promises."

"How much?" Fatima said.

"Sixty-five grand. I'm *pro bono*, but you'll need that much
for the application fees, fines, and the expeditor. And like
I told Mrs. Sykes on the phone, the minute he takes your
cash—and it's got to be cash—that's it. Win or lose, you
don't get it back."

"I appreciate your kindness," Fatima said, "but I will
never have that kind of money."

"We got it covered." Mom put a fat envelope on the
man's desk.

Fatima begged, "No."

"Yes," Mik said. "Let us do this. NaNa'll be so mad if you don't. She passed the hat at church. Everybody wants you here."

The church money would have covered only a bit of the cost. That and Joe Knows's money didn't add up to sixty-five thousand dollars. Mik and Mom had liquidated their savings. "I cannot let you do this," Fatima said.

"Make Brother Joe Knows happy, child," Mom said. "Make *us* happy. Fatima, this money? It's nothing until you let us put it to this."

The lawyer studied the three women. "I have a good feeling about this one. In a couple of weeks we should have a temporary stay of deportation that'll let you be here legally while the rest of the paperwork goes through. Between now and then, keep out of trouble. You get found out, Immigration considers you a criminal, and all bets are off. You'll never get back in. Beware of rats."

Fatima couldn't look at them. "I don't know how to thank—"

"Hush now," Mom said.

Mik nodded and put her finger to her lips.

"I'll give the expeditor the money tonight," the lawyer said. "Fatima, we'll start a regular application for your sister. It'll take a lot longer, but it'll cost a lot less, and you won't need money for that one for a few months. Now I have to ask you a tough question. Realistically, what are the chances she's still alive?"

"She is alive. She can be nothing else."

chapter 33
TAMIKA

Mik's lunch spot under the stairs, an ordinary Wednesday afternoon, 1:30 p.m., five hours before the hanging . . .

Text from Gale: OUT SICK. MISS ME?

Mik's lips wrinkled. She texted back: SORT OF, but didn't get to send the message.

A knotted scarf gagged her from behind. A paper bag covered her head. Seven or eight girls were on her. They bent her arms behind her back and dragged her downstairs into the school basement. Their laughter was muddy in her old hearing aids. The paper bag came off in the jostling. Somebody grabbed her hair and twisted it to keep her from turning around to see her attackers.

They dragged her to the custodian's room, shoved her into a mop closet and slammed the door. Her hand vibrated.

She'd been squeezing her phone the whole time. The display lit up with a text: SHA GONNA SMILEY U. A smiley was an ear-to-ear cut across the face.

She dialed 911, told the operator where she thought she was. The sound coming from her phone wasn't so much a voice as hiss and static. Ten minutes later she was past panic, wondering if the operator got the message. She banged on the inside of the closet door with her knees, her forehead. "I can't breathe. I can't breathe."

"And you couldn't see their faces?"

"No."

The principal nodded. "You have somebody to walk you home later?"

"My friend."

"Stop by my office on your way out. I'll wait with you till your pickup comes."

At three o'clock she went to the principal's office. The secretary said, "Somebody set off a cherry bomb in a toilet. He's out front with the police."

Mik headed for the exit. A girl cut her off, flashed a box cutter. Mik spun back for the principal's office. Another girl with a box cutter. The only way out was the back door. She ran for it, blasted into the garbage bay. Between the Dumpsters a third girl waited for her. Mik sprinted for the park woods. When she turned back, the three girls had become thirty. All were new recruits, girls not cool enough to be in Sha's previous crew. They were eager to please her with their chains and broken bottles. One of them threw a Coke can at Mik's head. It exploded on a tree in a spray of copper and quartz. They had filled it with rocks and pennies.

Mik stayed off the paths, weaving through the thorn wood and weed tree thickets for the cliffs. Fallen leaves covered vines that tripped her up. A bamboo forest broke through what had been a basketball court fifty years ago. Trashed mattresses littered the woods. Clouds capped the sky and buried any hint of sun. She had no bearing on west, the way home.

She didn't look back for a long time. Breathless, she stopped to turn on her hearing aids.

Punches of static croaked like a recording of the human voice slowed down. Mik recognized the sounds as engine noise from a 747 booming northwest out of LaGuardia. She found sky through a hole in the dead trees.

Yes, it was a plane.

Something bit her forearm just beneath the elbow. Her leather jacket was slashed, underneath that her sweatshirt. Underneath that was slick red. She felt no pain for a second, then a searing sting. What made her scream was the sight of all that blood dripping from her sleeve cuff.

Hard hands punched her from behind. She tripped over a dead log, spun as she fell to land faceup. The back of her head smacked the frosty dirt. The wind knocked from her, she gulped, sure she would choke on the acid in her throat.

Shanelle's knees pinned Mik's arms. A backhand slap

cracked Mik's face. Sha held her box cutter a shaky inch from Mik's eyes. "Read 'em: I win."

"Why?" Mik said. "Why you hate me?"

"Getting me suspended, turning my crew away from me? You stole my man."

"I didn't."

"*Meek*-a Sykes. Y'all are just too . . . "

"What?"

"Hell am I talking to you for?" Shanelle lifted the box cutter and swung down at Mik's cheek.

Mik shut her eyes.

Shanelle's weight lifted.

Mik opened her eyes.

Jimmi ducked. Shanelle slashed open his backpack. A coffee can spun from the bag and hit the ground with a small explosion of ash. Shanelle was fast with her cutter, but Jimmi's hands were faster. He ducked another swing, snatched Shanelle's arm, bent her wrist and dropped her with a leg sweep. He had her on her knees. "Don't make me break your arm," he said, something like that. Mik's heavy breathing overwhelmed her hearing aids. In her head she heard a saw ripping metal.

"You're a'ready breaking it! Dag junkie, leg*go*. Crazy Jimmi, I will *scream*!"

"You're already screaming." Jimmi pried the box cutter from Sha's clawed fingers, clicked the blade to safety, slipped it into his pocket. He released her. "Go. Run."

She did. She didn't look scared. She looked as if she wanted to blow up the world.

"Her posse was swarming the woods," Jimmi said. "I followed the racket. They're circling in from uphill." He had Mik up and running south for the road.

She couldn't catch her breath, was sure she would puke. She had to stop at the wood's edge. Her blood trickled onto the sidewalk.

Jimmi drew Shanelle's box cutter. He cut away Mik's sleeve at the elbow. Mik's skin pulled apart to expose the meat beneath. Jimmi took off his jacket, then his T-shirt. He cut the tee into strips and bandaged Mik's wound. "We get you to the hospital. I piggyback you."

He started up the road, stopped when he saw Shanelle and her posse rounding the corner. Mik on his back he ran downhill for the highway.

She thought she would throw up on him with all the bouncing.

More of Shanelle's crew cut them off downhill.

Jimmi ducked into a cut in the off-ramp wall. The rusted gate swung into the gray underneath the highway and then a stairwell. "Mik, your aids on?"

She groaned, "Yuh," the acid pushing into her mouth. Her wound throbbed.

"Might want to turn 'em off for this next bit. Just hang on to me. I got you. No fear."

They descended into darkness. The stairwell echoed screeches and booms from the trucks pounding the highway overhead. Sewer water charged fat pipes below. She didn't dare let go of him to turn off her aids. "Where we going, Jimmi?"

"Where they'll never find us."

The dark was absolute. She had no sense of distance. She could have been in a coffin or a void between galaxies. A train's hum and rattle echoed over the fading highway noise as they dropped deeper into the blackness.

Mik hyperventilated until she sensed she was slipping from Jimmi's back, falling. She passed out.

chapter 34
FATIMA

Bronx-Orange high school, the front
courtyard, two hours and forty minutes
before the hanging . . .

Fatima paced the sidewalk in front of the school. Mik was
nearly an hour late. Fatima approached the security guard.
He said he was pretty sure he hadn't seen Mik leave. He gave
Fatima a visitor's pass to the principal's office. The secretary said she was certain Mik had gone.

Fatima found a working pay phone and called Mik's
cell phone, no answer. She called the Sykeses' apartment.
The phone rang and rang.

She searched the streets in a panic. She and Mik were
supposed to teach today. Fatima hurried uphill toward
the VA.

chapter 35
TAMIKA

Jimmi's cave, fifty-six minutes before
the hanging...

She came to on a sleeping bag in a half-finished subway station lit blue by camp stove light. He'd left soup
and soda for her, and rebandaged her arm. She lifted the
gauze. He'd cleaned the wound and sealed it with what
looked like glue. Next to her lay an army pack full of
medical supplies: sterile dressings, peroxide, a ripped
packet of Dermabond adhesive, and morphine sticks.
One of the cases was cracked, the stick gone. She'd taken
morphine once, an IV drip when she was hospitalized a
few years ago for a serious ear infection. She was not on
morphine now.

Behind her in the stove light was a newspaper opened to
a full-page ad for travel to Costa Rica. Jimmi's words rode
the crinkles in the puffy clouds into the margins:

You're my angel, bomb blast bright,
No slight heaven, no minor light.
You are the way,
The truth,
The light.

How you love me, girl,
The world a swirl,
No way,
No truth,
No light?

Will you still love me,
When you find out I true be,
Outside humanity,
Lost with a fire's need,

A man from sands,
Forsaken plans,
No bonds or bands,
The Devil's hands?

Only you, child, can save me.

Just past the newspaper, in the dark, twin moths fluttered. No, eyes.

Mik rotated the stove to light them.

Jimmi sat against the wall, a spent morphine stick in hand. On the floor next to him was a silver gun.

"Sorry, Mik." He was pale, sweaty. He held up the morphine stick. "Forgot I had it. Needed just a little bit to take the edge . . . off." He pushed himself to his feet, tucked the gun into his belt.

"Jimmi—"

"I gotta find Fatima. She ain't safe up there with those girls and their box cutters about."

"I'm coming with you."

"No, kid. You're safe now. Down here, we're dead to the world. I'll come back for you." He drifted into the dark.

"Jimmi, please, don't leave me." Her voice box was knotted. No way he heard her.

She grabbed the stove by its handles and hurried into the tunnel. Jimmi was gone. She tried one offshoot tunnel, then another. She forced herself not to run, get lost, die in this maze. She checked her phone, no signal down here. She made her way back to the cave and balled up on the sleeping bag. She clicked off her aids to block out the stove lamp's hiss. She closed her eyes and hugged herself. She couldn't block out the chattering inside her head. She was shaking to break her teeth. She gritted them to keep from biting her tongue as she whispered, "Fatima, please, be okay."

chapter 36
MOM

Forty-nine minutes before the
hanging...

Sandrine Sykes mopped up a Target aisle. Some kid had
flipped a soda. Over the PA Sandrine's supervisor called,
"Drine S., please come to the manager's office. Immedi-
ately."

"What did I do wrong this time?" Drine muttered.

The manager met Sandrine halfway. "I'm so sorry, Drine."

"What?" Sandrine said. "Somebody's dead, right? Oh
God, don't tell me."

Half O House tower #4 crammed into the apartment.
Someone from NaNa's church led folks in prayer. Someone else yelled, "Y'all hush. Check it." The man dialed up
the TV volume.

The local newscaster said, "...abducted on her way

home from school by an emotionally disturbed veteran. What makes this story especially horrible is that Mika, as she is known to friends, is hearing impaired. Semprevivo is thought to be armed with a box cutter—"

"Turn it off," Drine yelled from the hallway. "Please, turn off the . . . sound."

Somebody muted the TV. In the hush, Drine Sykes backed into the bathroom and closed the door. Her back to the wall, she slid to the floor. The noise came back, the praying, the TV blasting the news.

A round of *Bless-eds* rang out from faraway, then muffled knocking on the bathroom door. This was it. Someone had come to tell her that her daughter had been raped and murdered and left a mangled corpse on the reservoir slope.

She watched the doorknob turn. NaNa's lips moved but no sound came from them.

NaNa closed the door and knelt before Drine to be at her eye level. She took Drine's hands away from her ears. NaNa's voice was soft but firm. " . . . onna be okay." NaNa held Sandrine's hands. Both women's hands seemed old for their age.

"Everybody says he's crazy."

"Everybody *says*, but nobody knows. But you and me, *we* know Jimmi since he was a kid now, don't we? We *know* him, Drine."

"He kidnapped my daughter. He's snapping. He's gonna—"

"No, he's not. He's not. Hush now. Sister Sykes, Jimmi would kill himself before he brought harm to Tamika. He brings a world of hurt unto himself, but his heart is pure with the Spirit. I come to you as truth's witness."

chapter 37
TAMIKA

Twenty-four minutes before the hanging . . .

Mik shivered in the tunnel draft. So much silence as the second hand on her watch clicked slower than the time it takes to cross one dead universe after another. Finally she felt the vibration. She clicked on her aids to confirm the tremors' source: skate wheels on cracked concrete.

An invisible fist broke into her abdomen, opened up with long hard fingers and squeezed her stomach.

Jimmi stepped off his board into the stove light.

"Thank you, Jimmi."

"For what?"

"You came back."

"Of course. Couple of Shanelle's crew still up there, hunting around by the highway. No sight of Fatima."

"You're a good man."

"Yeah? There's things y'all don't know about me. Mik, I watched people die over there. I didn't stop the killing."

"Jimmi, you didn't start it."

"I wonder, kid. I ask myself. Is it worth it, the living? Why bother, you know?"

"Sit with me. Give me that gun."

He did.

It was a lot heavier than she'd have thought. She set it behind her, pushed it out of reach. "Hold my hand. Without you, I wouldn't have met Fatima. Without you, Fatima wouldn't have met the kids at the hospital. Without you, people wouldn't have smiled that day you stood on the mailbox and set the angels flying."

"I just wanna be someplace bright and clean," he said.

"I'm-a take you there. Close your eyes. Squeeze my hand tight now, we gonna fly. If an ocean."

"If an ocean."

"Not the shore, Jimmi. The water. Not in it. Above it. We're dancing on it. We soaring now, thirty feet over the seas—"

"No land in sight, middle of the night, but lit bright, every star a kite, planets burning might."

Mik bopped her head to Jimmi's mix. "Nobody's uptight. There you go, man."

"People be playing, everybody saying, 'reeling this day in, to my heart, my heart, my heart.' Where we at now, Mik?"

"Oh we far, far out now, Jimmi. Just the warm wind and us. See them waves?"

"Big as countries. Rolling the moon. I'm reaching up—"

"Reach up, Jimmi."

"I'm grabbing two moonbeams."

"Outta sight."

"They're our surfboards, Mik."

"We *flying* off the top of that moon wave, man. We're *way* high now. The world's small. We in the sea of space."

"The sea of space."

"And the stars are our people. Everyone sparkles. Everybody you ever loved and who was kind to you is with us."

"Julyssa?"

"She's with us, Jimmi."

"My baby?"

"She's with us." Mik shut her eyes to see it all. "Out here the party goes on all night to the tune of a sweet-strummed guitar. There are no accidents out here. No injuries, no fighting, no hunger. When folks smile, you feel like they're hugging you. Out here promises are kept. The snow never turns to slush, nobody's sick, and everybody has a nice safe house and Moms doesn't have to work so hard and nobody's lonely and nobody fears and I can hear it all pain free." She opened her eyes.

Jimmi nodded. "What all you hear, angel?"

Mik smiled. "What's real."

chapter 38
JIMMI

The hanging . . .

Jimmi and Mik rushed through the streets toward the VA hospital where they would find medical attention and—please—Fatima teaching her class.

"If she's not there, we'll call my apartment," Mik said. "You got quarters? Lost my phone in the cave."

"Security guard'll let us use a phone," he said.

"After that, we check her house."

"After that, we call the cops."

"She'll freak, we get the police out looking for her."

"No choice. And anyway the police ain't mandatory reporters." Not yet, he almost said.

"You said Fatima and I were gonna create the most beautiful thing in the world," Mik said.

"You did."

"The Liberty we painted on the PD garage? It wasn't *that* good."

He shook no. "You still haven't figured it out. The bombs can fall and waste us, but what you two made will last forever."

"That's him, the dude on the TV," some cat said to his boy as Mik and Jimmi passed. The men were scoring malt forties on the tailgate of a parked car.

Jimmi followed the men's eyes to Mik's lips and cheek, swollen from when Shanelle clocked her. They stared at the blood-soaked bandage on her forearm. Then their eyes went to him.

Mik pulled him across the street. "We gotta hurry now, Jimmi."

He looked over his shoulder. Car doors were opening, tenement doors. Men followed, drawing their phones. Five dudes trailed them, eight, now a ninth with a Louisville Slugger.

"Jimmi, you run," she said. "You *fly*."

"I ain't leaving you," he said. The morphine had started to wear off. He would get her to the avenue, the traffic, people— "People, please," he said to the vigilantes.

They came down on him fast, tens of them, seeming like hundreds as they ripped Mik from him. Pinned against a truck, he could do no more than watch as they passed her kicking and screaming to an enormous woman who held her back with manlike arms. He broke free with a pair of punches that jacked the men into a fury. Their hatred stunned him. He knew these men, their brothers, mothers, sisters, daughters, helloed them daily in these streets surrounding the hospital. They were his neighbors, his friends. Why now did they kick him? He called out to them by name, and they struck him harder. He staggered to bent knees. "Let her go," he said. "Do what you got to do with me, but let her go."

Somebody kicked the back of his skull. Numbness spread over and through him.

"String 'im up," said the lead vigilante, some gang-banger.

They roped him by his ankles, threw the line over the streetlamp's arm and heaved him high. The physical pain was nothing compared to seeing them upside down with fever in their eyes. He'd seen men work each other up like this in battle. Any sense of why they were killing was lost to them. They knew nothing but a want for maximum destruction. One man saddled another's shoulders. Another handed that man the ball bat. He jabbed Jimmi's gut. More men saddled more shoulders and pummeled Jimmi Sixes. They beat his arms and legs, his face with fists that tore skin. One man lashed him with a studded belt.

Jimmi felt as if he'd been thrown under a speeding car. He convulsed. The rope snapped and dropped him to the sidewalk. Falling into darkness he saw Mik and thought, *I want to live. I was eighteen.*

chapter 39
TAMIKA

The fall . . .

Jimmi dropped onto the crowd. Landing on them made them angrier. They tossed him at each other as if he were somebody else's trash.

"What a sound," the leader said to Mik. "Somebody make that girl stop bawling."

The giant woman held her hand over Mik's mouth, jerking back just shy of hard enough to snap Mik's neck. She twisted Mik to make her see the woman's slitted eyes and pulled-back lips. "It's all right, baby. It's all right now," the woman said. When Mik bit the woman's palm, the bruiser jerked harder on Mik's head. "Hush. We got you. He can't hurt you now, blessed child."

"Roll 'im out," the lead gangbanger said. "Roll 'im *out*, I said. Yeah, like that. Put his chin on the curb and stomp down."

Two lifted their boots to kick down the deathblow to the back of Jimmi's neck when someone must have yelled something that got the men to hold up. They whipped their heads to look up the street. Mik followed their eyes.

"You will *stop*." Fatima shoved through the crowd. She put herself between Jimmi and the mob.

"Get that bitch out the way," the lead gangbanger said.

Others shouted the same and worse. The screaming shorted out Mik's hearing aids. She read one woman's lips: "Terrorist."

Fatima stood tall and spread out her hands stained with newspaper ink. She yelled to quiet the mob. As the crowd noise dropped off, Mik's hearing aids came back partway. Fatima said, "You will not harm this man. You will not."

"Move or die," the lead gangbanger said.

"Are you so anxious to hit a woman, great man? Are you so brave? I am sure the police will think so. What is the punishment for striking a child here? Where I come from they cut off your arms."

"Do 'im," the leader said to the posse. "Before the heat rolls up."

But Fatima stood firm, keeping herself between the men and Jimmi. "Will you put your hands on a *girl*?" she said.

A man reached for Jimmi. Fatima scratched his face. He backhanded her. Fatima made no effort to duck the shot. She wiped her mouth and held up bloody hands. "Do you see? This man has bloodied a child. Will you stand here and do nothing? Will you be accomplices to this crime? Will you?"

All snap-turned their heads downhill.

Sirens on the move bleated in Mik's ears.

"Grab 'im," the head dude said. "We'll bring 'im to my basement and finish it there."

But the crowd had started to bolt.

Red and blue flicker brightened on the buildings.

Mik looked out onto the sea of men, some anxious as they shoved to get out of the crowd, some near regret, some drunk and laughing. The gumball-colored lights from a dozen cop cars thickened on their faces.

Fatima stood over Jimmi. Her eyes hard, she signed to Mik, *GOOD-BYE*.

chapter 40
FATIMA

NYPD stationhouse, an hour and a half
later . . .

A cop brought them something to drink. "You sure you don't want to go the hospital?"

Fatima took the icepack away from her mouth, shook no, smiled. Mik too had refused medical attention, demanding to stay with Fatima.

"Just hang out here a few more minutes. Captain has a couple of questions. After that we'll drive you home." He pointed to Mik. "*Then* will you let us take you to the ER?"

Mik nodded.

The cop left them with a tin of peanuts.

"I am afraid of the captain's questions," Fatima said.

"I'm telling you, it's illegal for them to ask your immigration status," Mik said.

Mom came back. She had been talking with the police out in the hall. She closed the door and brought Fatima into a hug.

"Mom, what's wrong?" Mik said.

The door swung in. Two men in suits pushed past a cop trying to hold them back. The police captain followed them. He was angry.

One of the men flashed a badge: U.S. Department of Immigration. He said to Fatima, "I'll tell you flat out, I do not want to be doing this, especially after what I heard you did."

"Then why not take a walk and forget about it?" the police captain said.

"You know I can't do that," the federal agent said.

"How could you turn her in like that?" Mom said.

"We didn't," the captain said.

"Our reward money line got an anonymous tip about an illegal from a country on our terror watch list. The call triggered a priority check. The report has been filed. She's in the system now. Fatima, I'm sorry, but do you have any ID?"

Adjusting her hearing aids, Mik seemed to have a hard time taking in the many voices. "Who?" she said. "Who ratted her out?"

"No," Fatima said. "Do not tell me. I do not want to know." The room was cold but she was sweating.

chapter 41
TAMIKA

The emergency room, four hours later,
midnight . . .

Bloods and MS-13 were locked to chairs and bleeding after a brawl.

The nurse pointed to a curtained bay. NaNa was stroking Jimmi's hand, but he was out of it. The vigilantes had broken his nose, his teeth. The welts around his eyes were turning purple. Bandages covered his arms and shoulders where the men whipped him.

"Tamika, he was asking for you," NaNa said. "Even with the tranquilizers he was very agitated until I swore to him that you were safe."

Mom hesitated, went to Jimmi's bedside. "Jimmi? Thank you for taking care of Tamika. Jimmi?"

His eyes drifted to Mik. "I messed up, kid."

"No you didn't, Jimmi. You did great."

"They bring me in here, I'm asking for Fatima. I seen that dude backhanded her before I blacked out, she's bleeding from her mouth—"

"Easy now, Jimmi," Mom said.

"I'm on the cot, the pain, man, they got me hooked up to the morphine, I couldn't think right, I'm calling out to anybody who'll listen, 'Is Fatima okay? Somebody check on Fatima.' This old man come up to me, say he a priest, he gonna help me find Fatima, what's she look like, like that. I'm like, she's tall, pretty, scar over here, beautiful accent. I'm telling him about you too, so he can look for y'all, but all the old man wants to know is about Fatima's accent, what country. The painkillers, man, messing me up—I tell him where she's from. His eyes bug. Is she legal, he ask me."

"Oh God, Jimmi, please, no." Mom took his hand.

"By now I recognize him. He's that old dude works folks outside the supermarket with a beggar's cup, way lost junkie. The nurse come up to him, tell him she gonna call security if he don't leave, she warned him the last time, 'No more methadone for you tonight,' like that. He ain't listening to her, his eyes on me as he's backing away. I'm yelling at him, 'Yeah, course she's legal,' but it's too late. He's nodding, sad eyes desperate, on a scramble for the exit. He's one of them dudes always dialing 555-TIPS for reward money to raise cash for a score."

NaNa said, "Mmm. God save us. Mmm."

"Help me, Mik."

"Jimmi." Mik wiped the sweat from his face.

"Get me out of here, kid. Set me free." His eyelids fluttered. "If . . . I'm riding my skateboard, banging my sweet chords, rappin' like a street lord, Lord my sweet Lord, I ain't *ig*nored, this day a blue day, the essence of a true day, I'm riding, I'm riding, I'm flying . . ." He drifted to sleep.

That Friday was the day before what she was told would be her last time with Fatima. She had pled guilty and agreed to immediate expulsion to avoid fines and prison time.

Mik gathered the kids from the VA class and more than a few vets at the hospital basketball court. "We're gonna make a nice good-bye for Fatima. Something that'll last a while for when y'all shoot hoops, help you remember her maybe." She drew outlines onto the wall with Magic Marker and directed everyone where and how to fill them in. After a while the kids had to leave, but the vets stayed until the mural was done just before midnight. Mik had taken pictures of the kids and vets painting the wall. After everyone was gone, she took pictures of the finished mural.

She went home and downloaded the pictures. The hours passed too quickly as she cropped and printed the photos and pasted them into a book. She wrote captions beneath the photos, highlights from the students' good-bye notes. Some time after dawn, Mom's hands rested on Mik's shoulders.

"Ready?"

Mik didn't say.

chapter 42
FATIMA

Jersey City, a detention center,
Saturday morning...

The walls were painted glossy yellow, the chipped floor tiles too. The room was too big for the small table and two chairs. The sun shined hard through big windows. She squinted south through the glare. Behind the office buildings was the Statue of Liberty.

Fatima could see no more than the tip of the torch, washed out against the too blue sky.

The door opened. The guard explained that she could see only one visitor at a time. Mom came in, said, "Oh girl—"

"Mom, this is nothing, what will happen next," Fatima said. "Please, do not worry."

"But what will you do?"

"I have so many friends, Mom. They in the camps will rejoice at my homecoming. With the sign my sister Mik taught me, they will ask me to lead a new school. There are many who will be eager to know what I have learned here. This is a remarkable opportunity for me. I will send you many letters and tell you of my progress."

"Fatima, my child."

chapter 43
TAMIKA

The waiting room . . .

Mik took out her old aids, put in her new ones. She didn't turn them on.

Mom came out looking weary, but she straightened up with a bright face when she saw Mik. She nodded that Mik should go in.

Fatima waited by the window. "Sister Mik."

Mik nodded.

Fatima signed, THANK YOU FOR BEING MY FRIEND.

Mik pushed the photo book across the table. The guard had checked it for weapons, razor blades.

Fatima opened the book. She took in each picture, each student's good-bye. She turned the page to the last photo, a wide-angle shot of the mural. Newsprint people strolled amongst stars and planets. It lit Fatima up. "What do you call it, this fantastic dream?"

Mik clicked on her new aids. There was a hum, distant plane noise. Closer was the sound of breathing, Fatima's, hers. "If an Ocean."

Fatima sized up the photo of the painted skyscape, nodded. "Good." She hugged the book to her. "I must ask you a favor." Fatima's voice was softer and more delicate than Mik would have imagined.

Mik nodded.

"Every Third?"

"I went by twice, waited, he never came."

"He must be hiding in the weeds. Try the cat box. Put a few paper mice in it. He likes to bat them around. He will come to you. The cold is upon us. He knows it is time to come inside. Mik, I figured it out. The project Jimmi said we were working on? The most beautiful thing in the world? He meant friendship. Sister, this is a lovely country. You have peace here. One needs only a little food, a warm place to sleep and dream, and someone with whom she can share a laugh. I was most fortunate to know these three beauties. They will last forever." She worked up her fantastic smile. "Besides, I will be back."

"Promise me."

"I have a present for you too." She slid two tiny silver suns across the table, rays curled. "Earrings, but you will need to put them on posts. I was not allowed to have metal in my room this morning. They are only folded Wrigley's wrappers, but do you like them?"

Mik held them to her lobes. "How they look?"

"Now they are pretty."

The door opened. "Sorry, but it's time." The guard stepped outside, left the door open.

"Sister Mik, when I was a child, my mother took us on a long journey and we swam in the Nile. The winds blew the grasses for miles, and from the grasses a little bird sang my name. I have known such things, just as I know we will see each other again, okay? I will come back with my sister, and we will get all that paint from the ghost house and paint the street a rainbow." She laughed as she signed HELLO, GOOD-BYE, I LOVE YOU. She hugged Mik quickly, broke away and left the room fast without looking back.

chapter 44
FATIMA

The sky, Saturday afternoon ...

Out of Newark, the plane flew east. She imagined her sister welcoming her at the camp gates, her arms wide, fists raised in unbeatable glee.

Over the PA system, the captain said, "If you look to your left, you'll see the Statue of Liberty facing us."

Fatima watched until the plane was closest to Liberty, and then she closed her eyes so her Mother of Exiles would never fade into the distance.

chapter 45
TAMIKA

East of the Orange Houses, late
Saturday afternoon . . .

She studied what she and Fatima had painted over the
abandoned garage. Already the taggers had hit Liberty with a beard and turned the torch into a screw you
salute.

She found the key under the mat but didn't need it.
Fatima had left the door open.

She readied the cat box with paper mice, threw in some
cheese. At sunset the rickety cat came back. He bunched
himself between Mik's feet. He made weak attempts to
scratch her but gave up fast and let himself be put into the
box.

Mik looked around the room for anything else she

should take. Fatima had nothing, only the newspaper dolls.

Mik left and left the door open for the wind to take the dolls.

On the way home she passed the bodega. FOR RENT in the window, the joint was stripped. The only trace of Joe Knows was the store's sign, Tranquilito's. Somebody was taping flyers to the glass: DID YOU KNOW THAT YOU COULD MAKE 5-10K/MONTH WORKING AS AN INFORMATION SPECIALIST FOR THE US DEPT OF IMMIGRATION?

Downhill by the highway an old woman sold newspapers from Fatima's spot.

The next day Mik went to the hospital. Jimmi was AWOL.

She convinced Gale to go with her down into Jimmi's cave. Their flashlights found Mik's phone but no sign of Jimmi.

She tried the VA. "Nope," George, the head volunteer dude, said. "Hey, you did a good job that time, with the kids. How'd you like to take over Fatima's class?"

Mik stuck her hands into her back pockets, shrugged. "Sounds good."

The next Wednesday she was hanging with Gale in the school yard. She scratched her arm where Shanelle cut her. Sha was back in juvie for aggravated assault. The Gang Intelligence Unit had busted up her crew. She wouldn't be bothering Mik anytime soon.

"Any word from Fatima?" Gale said.

"Phones are all messed up over there. She'll write soon. She will."

Gale nodded. "You all right?"

"Better when I'm around you."

"That sounds like a marriage proposal," he said.

"In your craziest dream."

"That's right."

Thanksgiving . . .

The rain stopped at twilight. Mom took the ice packs off Mik's ears, pierced the lobes and helped Mik get Fatima's earrings into the holes.

Mik checked herself in the mirror, the twin silver suns at her cheeks. "Big ears I got," she said.

"You're beautiful," Mom said.

She went to show NaNa, but she was asleep on the couch.

Mik went to her room, sat cross-legged on her bed. She thumbed through the pictures on her phone—goofy snaps of Fatima on the Statue of Liberty ferry.

Outside the window, thunderheads kicked across the sky as fast as the cars on the highway.

The cat's purring was nice in her new hearing aids. Across the breezeway some old dude was playing sax in his kitchen. Folks argued, TVs screamed commercials, police helicopters chucked. The world was loud, no doubt about that. She thought maybe she could get used to it.

Mom watched her from the door.

"Yo, Ma, you think you can see your way to playing that guitar?"

To tune it took a minute. Mom dropped her hand and a fuzzy chord, winced. A few minutes later she was strumming. She didn't sound great. She sounded good.

Tamika Sykes heard it clearly: laughter, her mother's, her own.

Laughter out on the strip, a lone voice . . .

Down in the street, his filthy clothes rippling in the wind, Jimmi Sixes wandered into the courtyard on shaky legs, his face scabbed. He laughed at the night. "The highway's clanging, wind's fingers jangling, people be moving, everybody grooving, all the world flowing, hush-n-rush blowing, I-87, road to all heavens, freeway lights passion, cars trucks flashing, sound of waves crashing." He clapped his hands, yelled to no one, "Yeah, baby. That's how we bang it out here in the Orange Houses."

"I better call the ambulance." Mom put the phone to her ear. "How that Jimmi does go on and on."

"Yeah," Mik said. "Will you listen to him?"

thank you . . .

Kate, for your kindness, generosity, vast knowledge, the most gorgeous notes and your all-around magnificence. You are too wonderful, and I am too lucky to get to write for you. Thank you for taking these stories—and me—under your wing.

Lauri, aka Ms. Amazing, for your remarkable and formative notes and for making Dial such a beautiful place to be. You are too good to me.

Shelley, Liz, Alisha and Jess for the time you took to read drafts and give brilliant notes; Regina, Jasmin and Kristin for your absolutely inspiring work; Steve, Scottie, Emily, Julianne and Donne for backing the book; Penny, Michael, Anne and all the great folks at Text for your enthusiasm.

Kirby, consigliere and true pal, Richard Abate, Mike Harriot, David Vigliano, Lynn Pleshette and Rowan Riley.

Scott Smith, the most awesome writer, mentor and generous soul.

The lovely Nan Mercado, Richie Partington, David Levithan and Angela Carstensen for all you do for YA readers.

My families and super-cool mothers, JG, Matt, Kari and Billy for your excitement; Kath and Marie Mordeno for your hilarious phone calls and relentless pimping; Pop, for reading all those manuscripts gathering dust in my closet as if they weren't completely horrible, and for encouraging me with always thoughtful notes and otherworldly wisdom.

Risa, for making the world go 'round.

"Fatima," for talking and walking with me that clear, late April day when the ginkgo buds were breaking around the Jerome Park Reservoir.

And

Robyn, for putting heart and soul into this story, teaching me what it is about and bringing so much to it, including its title; and for giving that first draft of *TMR* to Nancy and Lauri. You are a phenomenal editor and friend, and you're in my heart forever.

THE ORANGE HOUSES
DISCUSSION QUESTIONS

- What was it like to read this story knowing that a hanging was coming up? How did the author build suspense even though you knew that something terrible was going to happen?

- What did you think about Mik, Fatima, and Jimmi? What did you think about Shanelle, Jaekwon, and The G? Would you be friends with any of these characters?

- Is anyone a hero in this story? Who and why? Or, why not? What is heroism? Is anyone a victim in this story? Explain.

- What is Jimmi's *If* game? How does it help him? What is your If?

- What does this book say about illegal immigration? War?

- Fatima tells NaNa that she is not Muslim and not Christian, but human (page 40). What do you think this means?

- On page 45 the narrator tells us that Mik "hated when folks felt sorry for her, but she liked to feel sorry for other folks." What does she mean? What do you think about this idea? Do you feel sorry for anyone in this book?

- Why does Mik feel uncertain about having the operation or getting better aids to help her hear better? Do you understand her reasons? Do you agree? Why does she change her mind at the end and turn on her new hearing aids? How does Mik change from the beginning to the end of the story.

- When Jimmi leaves Mik and NaNa instead of letting them take him back to the hospital, NaNa tells Mik, "Only he can stop him" (page 103). What does she mean? Do you agree? Explain. Do you think they should have tried to make Jimmi go back to the hospital? Is there ever a reason a friend or relative should try to take care of someone against his or her own wishes? Explain.

- What do you think motivated Shanelle to be angry at Mik? Why do you think Shanelle had a posse? Is there anything that would help Shanelle? Explain.

- Why did NaNa and Drine have different opinions of Jimmi? What's the difference between saying and knowing, as NaNa talks about on page 123?

- What is a vigilante? What do you think about what the neighborhood people did to Jimmi? Would it have made a difference if Jimmi had done what the television news reported? Explain.

- Fatima's mother told her daughters "This is nothing, what will happen next. This is nothing" when she led the men away to keep her children safe (page 56). Fatima says the same thing to Drine when she is about to be sent back to the refugee camps (page 138). What did they each mean? Why did they say this?

• Why did Jimmi get beaten up? Why did Fatima get detained by immigration officials? Who do you blame for what happened in this story? Was there anything that one or more of the characters could have done differently that would have changed the course of the events in this book? Explain.

• Do you think the United States is a lovely country? Is it peaceful? Why or why not?

• Fatima says that Jimmi meant friendship is the most beautiful thing in the world (page 141). What do you think about this idea? What is true friendship? On the same page, Fatima also talks about what a person needs. Do you agree with her shortlist? What would you say a person needs? What is the difference between need and want?

• What does this story say about people making assumptions? Does this story make you rethink your assumptions about someone you know? Explain.

• What do you think happens to Mik? Fatima? Jimmi? Shanelle? What are they each doing in ten years?

• What will you remember from this book? Would you recommend it to others? What would you tell them about it?

Turn the page

for an excerpt from Paul Griffin's

TEN MILE RIVER

1

RAY WAS BIGGER but José was boss. They were fourteen and fifteen, on their own and on the run.

José pulled two lead pipes from the knapsack he made Ray wear, slapped one into Ray's hand. "Shut your eyes before you smash the glass."

"You said the same damn thing last time."

"And you forgot to do it last time." José smacked the back of Ray's giant head.

They were hiding in the park. Ray studied the three-quarter moon spraying light they didn't need.

"Let's git to work," José said.

They made their way through the weed trees, downhill toward their target, a line of parked cars. José peeled off his shirt, wrapped it around his arm. He was skinny, ripped. "Strip off that shirt, Ray-Ray."

1

"I'm a'right." Ray's pipe slipped out of his sweaty hand, rang on the sidewalk. "Quit lookin at me like I'm a moron."

"You *are* a moron."

"Think I dropped it on purpose?"

"With you, you never know." José hustled ahead.

Ray eyed the tenements, the air conditioners hanging lopsided from windows. He worried one would fall someday, kill some kid in a stroller.

José never seemed to worry about what rotten thing might happen next. He gripped the pipe good, closed his eyes, swung down on an Escalade. The windshield imploded.

Ray smashed the far side of the street. There were a few jacked-up SUVs but mostly rear-ended Accords, gypsy hack Tauruses, poor folk rides. "Goddammit," Ray said. He knew he was breaking more than glass.

After they popped thirty-some windshields, lights and sirens spun a half mile up the road. The boys hid in the woods. José said, "That Escalade goes for eighty grand. All that bling, they deserve it."

They don't, Ray didn't say. Nobody does, not the poor folk, not the pimps neither. "Punks, every last one of 'em."

José poked Ray's gut. "A man's gotta eat, right, kid? Yo, after we get our bread, let's go boost us some DVDs. Gonna get me the *Goodfellas* deluxe."

"You got *Goodfellas* deluxe in your stack twice, still in the wrappers."

"Then I'm-a swipe me that other one," José said. "That

2

Godfather dude, homeboy never got his shirt on the whole movie. 'My name es *Tony* Mon*tana*.' That Scarface was a first-rate thug, them model-lookin chicks hangin half-nekkid around that dope swimmin pool he got out back his mansion there." José leveled his window-breaking pipe Uzi style at Ray. "'Say hullo to my lil' friend!'" He purred *rat-a-tat-tat* as he sprayed Ray with invisible bullets.

Ray couldn't make the *rat-a-tat-tat* sound, came back with a lame *ka-click* as he mimed lock and load, gave José the gory glory he wanted.

José danced like Tony Montana gobbling up machine gun fire at the end of *Scarface,* the kingpin stoked on coke as if he'd sucked dry a generator big enough to power the city. Ray played along, body slammed the J-man. José flipped and pinned his boy, never mind Ray had J by four inches and seventy pounds. If life ever boiled down to a face-off Ray could check-'n'-deck the J-man in one throw. Not that Ray knew this yet.

"You got cut," José said.

"Scratch is all."

José grabbed Ray's arm, checked out the cut. "It's not bad."

"Gimme back m' arm."

"I tolt you to wrap yourself, kid. How come you ain't take off your shirt?"

Ray looked away, shrugged. "Was cold."

"*Right.* Idiot." José eyed Ray. "You did real good back there. Let's get paid."

They worked their way through the woods to Van Cortlandt Park South and Jerry's Auto Glass, Best in The Bronx, the closest windshield fix for the thirty-some smashed cars. Jerry picked his teeth. " 'Sup boys?"

"You're up early, Jerry," José said.

"Thinkin I'm gonna be busy today." Jerry nodded at a banner strung over the garage bays: TODAY ONLY, 20% DISCOUNT.

"Might as well've had us put flyers under the windshield wipers," José said.

"Except there's no more windshields to put them flyers on, right, Slick?"

José nodded. "Howzabout our money?"

Jerry twirled his ear hair, sniffed his waxy fingers. "Howzabout how many?"

"Thirty-some," José said.

"That's good. Thirty-some shields is good." From a wad in his chest pocket Jerry flipped José a hundred.

"Buck fifty, we said," José said.

"See, here's the thing." Jerry took out his fake teeth to get rid of a string of food. "I'm short right now."

"You're short all the time," José said.

Jerry was short. He didn't like short jokes. "And you're funny, till I stab you."

"You stab me in a *dream* you better run," José said.

Jerry laughed, sounded like a car that couldn't get started. "You can't be fifteen, either of yous."

4